MCCRACKEN

AND THE

LOST ISLAND

By Mark Adderley

Scriptorium Press

Yankton, South Dakota

2013

Published by Scriptorium Press,
Yankton, South Dakota

McCracken

AND THE

Lost Island

Just then, the passage opened out into a wide cave. It had a lake in its middle, though this was a lake of molten rock, and it cast a lurid light over the walls and roof. In the middle of the lake was a stone structure, about twenty feet wide, a roof supported by two lines of Minoan columns. There was a jumbled collection of objects on the floor, objects I couldn't identify at this distance. A path led across the lake of fire to steps that ascended to the entrance of the structure—temple or whatever, it was impossible to say.

And there, outlined against the red glow of the lake, stood a terrible shape, resembling a man but stooped like an ape and with an oversized, horned head. It was the very picture of a fiend.

Without thinking, I leveled my revolver, took aim, and fired . . .

Also by Mark Adderley

The Hawk and the Wolf
The Hawk and the Cup
The Hawk and the Huntress

For Young Readers:
McCracken and the Lost Valley
McCracken and the Lost Mountain (forthcoming)

To Will and Nick,
Whose Idea It Was

Contents

Chapter 1. A Meeting in Africa 9

Chapter 2. The Lost Island 21

Chapter 3. Journey on an Airship 30

Chapter 4. Searching the Seabed 45

Chapter 5. The Underwater Temple 55

Chapter 6. The Exploration Begins 66

Chapter 7. The Island Moves 77

Chapter 8. The Temple of the Minotaur 90

Chapter 9. Fetching the fire stones 104

Chapter 10. Adventures in the Lake 117

Chapter 11. A Trek through the Marshes 130

Chapter 12. Descent into the Caves 139

Chapter 13. Labyrinths and Lava 154

Chapter 14. Doubling Back 168

Chapter 15. Pistols at Dawn 181

Chapter 16. A Diplomatic Solution 192

From Fritz's Kitchen 200

Chapter 1
A Meeting in Africa

It was the early summer of 1913, and I was returning from a safari—as I remember, we had bagged a couple of lions, a rhino and a number of zebras—when I saw a motor-car trundling towards us over the veldt. It was a brand-new Daimler, a twenty-horse-power, four cylinder beauty, with a high bonnet, silver body-work and red leather upholstery. It sent up clouds of reddish dust behind it, and the driver, peering short-sightedly through his goggles and occasionally wiping the veldt from them, stabbed repeatedly at his horn. When the car reached our caravan, it wheeled around so it was facing the same way as our horses.

"Herr McCracken?" asked the passenger in something of a German accent—a round man. He seemed to be all circles: round, bald head, round belly, pudgy fingers, horn-rimmed glasses that in the bright African sunlight seemed to be a pair of circular mirrors reflecting more of my eyes than revealing his.

I pulled the bandana from my nose, pushed the pith-helmet up an inch, and said, "I'm McCracken. Who might you be?"

The man thrust his fat hand out of the motor-car. "My name," he said, "is Friedrich Ludwig von Helleher-Stauffen, and very much at your service I am, Herr McCracken."

I shook hands with him—not an easy thing to do, matching the speed of my mount to the Daimler, which puttered along, occasionally spouting black smoke from its exhaust-pipe. In truth, the horse was a little skittish at the closeness of the motor-car, and it wasn't a real hand-shake—I got the impression of a sweaty palm and fingers that pressed mine only briefly.

"A proposal for you I have," said Helleher-Stauffen.

"Well, I'm always open to proposals," I replied, "just as soon as I get these carcasses to Marsabit and get cleaned up."

"Far across this desert I have driven, Herr McCracken," said the chap in the motor-car. "To you this matter I could disclose, should you wish it, now."

"McCracken!" came a voice. I turned to see my guide, Ngugi, hurrying his horse along to catch up

10

with me. He was chattering urgently in Bantu and pointing off to the left.

"I see it," I said to Ngugi.

"This proposal, Herr McCracken—" began Helleher-Stauffen.

"One moment," I said, holding up a hand to stop him and reaching for my elephant-gun with the other. I unslung it in a moment, and tossing the reins to Ngugi, I slipped down from the saddle and crept forward, cocking the gun as I went.

There it was: a bull elephant, ancient, in its last months. It looked miserable, the poor creature, and wandering in its wits. Its belly was hollow, its eyes sunken. Their teeth get ground down if they live too long, and they can't eat properly. Its destiny was a long, agonizing death by starvation.

Or it could provide me with a little ivory to trade.

Slowly, I raised the gun and fitted the stock to my shoulder.

"This proposal, Herr McCracken, concerns your fire stone," said a German voice.

Simultaneously, the elephant gun exploded, the bullet flew through the top branches of a tree, scattering leaves and twigs in all directions, and the elephant trumpeted and stomped away, vanishing in a cloud of dust kicked up by its own ponderous feet. I lined up for a second shot, but it had its back turned to me, and I couldn't be sure of dropping it.

Slowly, I got to my feet, quivering with rage. Helleher-Stauffen spread his hands. "My deepest apologies, Herr McCracken," he said. "But, after all, what is two pieces of indifferent ivory, when compared with . . . hm, how is it you would say in English? . . . vast treasure?"

"Vast treasure?" I repeated, doubtfully.

"*Ja*, Herr McCracken, vast treasure on . . . ah . . . *Verlorene Insel*. The lost island."

"I don't have the faintest idea what you're talking about. But that—" I jabbed my thumb over my shoulder. "That I understand—the elephant that got away. I understand how many pounds, real pounds, I could have got for his tusks, Mr. Hellehofen, or whatever your name is. Currently pounding away across the veldt are real pounds. That's real—a hundred pounds for—" I stopped. I'd been going to say, *for the Consolata Sisters*, the local Catholic missionaries, but I got the impression this fellow wouldn't understand. "Vast treasure on a lost island," I said, "isn't real." I suddenly realized what he had said earlier. "What about my fire stone?" I asked. "How do

12

you know about that? What has it got to do with anything?"

The German chuckled. "Very much, Herr McCracken, very much indeed. I too in Marsabit have taken a room, I and my three companions. You have heard of Vasili Sikorsky, of course?"

"Of course." Who hadn't heard of Vasili Sikorsky, the aviator? Only a couple of weeks earlier, he had flown the first ever four-engined aircraft, the *Russky Vityaz*, or Russian Knight. It was hinted that the Knight could move seven passengers a hundred miles at an operational ceiling of nearly two thousand feet. Only something truly important could have pulled him away from his passenger aeroplane at this time.

"You have perhaps also heard of Nicolas Jaubert?"

"Jaubert is here too?"

"*Ja*, Herr McCracken."

Jaubert had been developing a way of re-absorbing the carbon-dioxide breathed out by deep-sea divers, so that they could stay below for longer periods. I was beginning to be impressed.

"And, of course, you know Fraulein Ariadne Bell?"

"Of course I do," I spat back. "But if you know about my fire stone, you should know other things about me. It was unwise of you to bring her along if you want a favour from me."

Again, the German gave a chuckle. "Herr McCracken, you must . . . how is the phrase? . . . forget and forgive. Fraulein Bell, you might recall, is an expert in ancient languages, and has moreover been working on the problem of efficient wireless communication systems."

"A flyer, a diver, a communications expert. You have a significant part of a team."

"And an *engineer*, Herr McCracken."

I shrugged. "Perhaps you have an engineer," I said. "Perhaps not."

"Your work on the portable water turbine, Herr McCracken, it could be of inestimable value to us," said the Baron. "But it is not I who expect you to say yes. Our proposal you must hear in the first place, *ja*?"

"*Ja*, Herr Heller—Huffler-stuff . . . er . . . "

"Helleher-Stauffen. But you may call me the Baron, Herr McCracken," chuckled the German.

"Baron it is, then," I said. "I suppose I must hear your proposal, as you say. Where are your rooms in Marsabit?"

14

Again, that chuckle. "It is at the airfield I stay, Herr McCracken. Come with me you must, and all you will understand."

And so I went with him. I've always been a sucker for mysteries.

Marsabit is a thriving market town, the capital of the district, and the starting-point for any number of safaris and expeditions into the bush. All of this is as much as to say, it's a single road of red dust thrusting straight through a shabby collection of lean-tos. The fanciest building in the town is the post office, which looks like my grandma's house, except they paint it a bit brighter than she did.

All the hills round about, including Mount Marsabit, the extinct volcano, are covered with trees. But Marsabit is as dry as electricity, though it's not as clean. There's always a cloud of red dust hanging on the air. I know that there are at least two lakes on Mount Marsabit—old craters that have filled with rainwater—but none of that water makes it to the town. I've often wondered why they didn't build the town on the mountain.

To the north-east of the town, and out of it a fair step, is the aerodrome. It's just a strip of flat road-way with a shack and a wind-sock, but it serves. It brings rich men in to hunt, and it takes rich men and

15

occasionally their trophies back to a big city like Nairobi or Mombasa.

While the bearers were unloading the quarry at the office, I got a lift from the Baron. I've got to admit, it was a fine experience, bouncing along, my bones rattling like ball-bearings in an empty can, the wind whipping through my hair. But as we neared the aerodrome, I got interested in something else: a sleek, silver-grey object that lay along the red dust of the desert. Its top half reflected the cobalt blue of the sky, its underside the Martian red of the desert. It was at least four hundred feet long, like a huge pencil lying where some giant draughtsman had dropped it.

"Baron, is that what I think it is?" I asked.

"*Ja*, Herr McCracken," responded the Baron. "You like, yes? It was called the LZ3, or *Luftschiff Zeppelin 3*—Graf von Zeppelin's experimental airship. Now, it is LS3, the *Luftschiff Stauffen 3*."

"He was having some problems, I heard."

"Minor problems only, Herr McCracken, I assure you. The LS3 is innovational—it has stronger girders within the envelope, unlike the Graf's unfortunate LZ1. And it has elevators—they are flaps, that control—"

"Flaps that control the pitch of the aircraft—would that be them at the rear, Baron?"

16

"It is the stern you mean, Herr McCracken," chuckled the Baron. "Nautical terminology we use—fore, aft, port, starboard. It is—how is it you say?—more efficient."

"Yes, it would be."

"In fact, in an emergency, the whole gondola can detach from the envelope, and serve as a ship. The engines will lower, and propel it through water as well as it had been propelled through the air."

"Ingenious."

"This model the German Army bought from the Graf—he is a personal friend of mine—but I have obtained it from them, and made certain modifications."

"Like the gondola?" I asked, pointing at the long windowed cabin, like an ocean liner, protruding below the envelope.

"*Ja*, the gondola, Herr McCracken. You see, it is many times larger than the gondolas of previous airships. At eight hundred and fifty metres we can cruise, and over one thousand kilometres we can fly before it is needful to refuel. Here I leave, I refuel in Khartoum, in Luxor, in Cairo, and then . . . well, that really depends on you, Herr McCracken."

The chauffeur brought the Daimler to a sliding stop in a cloud of dust before the gondola. It was actually twenty feet above the ground, secured fore and aft with cables, but a set of portable steps had been wheeled against the door. We ascended and, stooping (it was nautical in all ways), entered.

A short passage—a couple of doors on one side, windows looking out at Mount Marsabit on the other—took us to the stern of the gondola, the *Speiseraum*, he called it. The first thing you noticed as you walked into this *Speiseraum* was that you were surrounded by windows. The great curved wall, which was also the very stern of the airship's gondola, was constructed from a series of windows, giving a 180-degree view of Marsabit—in flight, it would give you a wonderful panoramic view of where you had just come from. The room contained half a dozen teak tables, around which were drawn leather-backed chairs. The flat wall, where there were no windows, was a bar, stocked from floor to ceiling, and staffed by the chauffeur, pulling off his goggles. He was a short, red-haired and wall-eyed man, who seemed to drag one of his feet slightly. His face was still covered with dirt, but there were clean circles about his strange eyes.

"May I present Fritz, my servant," said the Baron. "Everyone else, Herr McCracken, you either know or can guess at."

For sitting or standing at the tables or by the windows were the three the Baron had mentioned: Vasili Sikorsky, the tall, heavily-built Ukrainian with blue eyes and golden hair—he looked more German than the Baron; Nicolas Jaubert, wiry, slim, and not much over five feet in height; and, by the window, sipping a tall glass of champagne and pretending she hadn't seen me, Ariadne Bell. I won't describe her. The world knows her dark-haired, dark-eyed beauty—none more than I.

"*Bonjour*, Monsieur McCracken!" cried Jaubert, setting aside his cognac and kissing me on both cheeks. Sikorsky nodded a greeting, snapping his heels together.

"Jaubert, I'm glad to make your acquaintance at last," I said. "Have you resolved the problem with the carbon-dioxide absorption?"

"*Oui, monsieur*," replied Jaubert. "It was in the end a matter so simple. I have a pair of prototypes on board, my rebreathers. It is with pleasure I look forward to using it on this expedition, yes?"

"Very exciting indeed," I said; and perhaps it will be, I thought. "Sikorsky," I said, holding out my hand. The Ukrainian clasped it firmly and shook. "I read about your success with the *Russky Vityaz*. My congratulations, sir."

19

"*Spassiba*, Mr. McCracken. And my congratulations to you on development of portable water turbine."

I nodded my thanks. "And how are the Romanovs?" I asked.

Sikorsky shook his head. "His majesty still grieves bitterly over the goldfield massacre," he said mournfully.

"It was a bad business," I commented. "I hope he can get over it." Slowly, I turned. I hadn't looked forward to this part. "Hello, Ari," I said, steeling myself for her onslaught.

"I want you to know," she said, turning to face me down with those dark, stormy eyes, "that I was against bringing you on this expedition at all, Mac." With that, she turned her back on me. I was struck by how perfectly formed her shoulders were.

"A drink, Herr McCracken?" suggested the Baron. "Your preference is whisky, I believe?"

"It is," I said, taking the glass from him—just how I like it, no water, no ice, just the good stuff.

"And now, it is to business we go," said the Baron gleefully and, rubbing his hands together, he brought out a map.

CHAPTER 2

THE LOST ISLAND

The four of us gathered eagerly around the map, and pored over it. Ariadne was the first to straighten up, puzzled, a single wrinkle appearing in her perfect nose. "That's just a map of the Mediterranean," she observed—rather unnecessarily, I thought.

"*Ja, ja*, Fraulein Bell," said the Baron gleefully. "*Mittelmeer*, the Middle Sea. Nothing unusual you see, *nicht wahr*?"

"It looks like an old map," I said—and it did. The paper was yellowed, the edges dark and crumbling. In fact, looking closer, I doubted that it was paper at all. Rubbing the edge between my fingers, I asked, "Parchment?"

"Vellum," Ariadne corrected me, without looking up from her examination of the map.

"This is not an original map, you understand, Herr McCracken," said the Baron, the teeth showing beneath his upper lip. "It was copied from a copy, which was copied from another copy . . . "

I grunted. "I'd say there was plenty of room for error there."

"On the contrary," said Ariadne, again without looking up from the map. "It was common until the invention of the printing press—the scribes and artists were extremely well trained. They made errors, but not nearly so often as you would think."

"And if you look carefully, Herr McCracken," said the Baron, "you will see that it is surprisingly accurate."

We all leaned over and examined the map more closely. I was looking at Italy, and wondering if it didn't lean just a little too much eastwards, when Ariadne said, "What's that large island north of Crete?"

The Baron chuckled. "*Genau*, indeed, Fraulein Bell. What is the island north of Crete?"

All eyes riveted on it: sure enough, there it was. Some forty miles north of Crete lay an island, about fifty miles across. It was circular—perfectly circular—with no detail marked on it at all, just a bull's head picked out in brown ink in the centre. I had at first mistaken it for a compass-rose.

While we were still marveling at this, the Baron snapped his fingers, and the red-haired bartender came slouching over. "Fritz, bring me my Plato!"

"*Jawohl, mein Herr!*" said Fritz, slouching off with some rapidity.

"A stupid fellow," the Baron remarked, when Fritz was barely out of the door, "and slow, but occasionally useful."

"*Très merveilleux, monsieur*," said Jaubert. "It is many times I have been swimming in these waters. I know many of the islands well. I know nothing of this large island."

"Almost two thousand years before the birth of Christ," the Baron explained, drumming his finger-tips together in delight, "a volcano precisely there erupted, leaving what had been one large island mere fragments. What had been a rich and sophisticated civilization sank beneath the waves, leaving only the mountain-tops exposed." He made a dismissive gesture. "This is all a matter of historical record."

"*Da*," said Sikorsky. "Of this volcanic eruption much I have heard. Its magnitude was like eruption of Krakatoa, thirty years ago, perhaps greater."

"The effects were felt as far away as China," said the Baron. "The sky darkened with the debris tossed up into the stratosphere. Crops failed. Civilization failed."

We all bent again over the map again, and a few moments later, puffing with the exertion, Fritz returned with a leather-bound volume that the Baron took wordlessly and started leafing through. "And, Fritz?"

"*Mein Herr*?"

"Coffee for everyone."

"*Jawohl, Mein Herr.*"

For a few moments, the Baron continued to leaf through the book, until Fritz brought the coffee. At length, the Baron looked up. "This is from Plato's

Timaeus," he said pedantically, and then began to read, carefully:

"It is related in our records how once upon a time Athens stopped the advance of a mighty army, which, starting from a distant point in the Atlantic ocean, was insolently advancing to attack the whole of Europe and Asia. The ocean there was at that time navigable; for in front of the channel which you Greeks call the Pillars of Heracles, there lay an island larger than Libya and Asia together. Now in this island, named Atlantis, there existed a confederation of kings, of great and marvelous power, which held sway over all the island, and over many other islands also and parts of the continent. They enjoyed all manner of wealth, obeying the laws of the gods, and for many centuries they knew that they could only have the true use of riches by not caring about them. But gradually they began to degenerate, though to the outward eye they appeared as glorious as ever. Then all-seeing Zeus, wanting to punish them, sent forth his thunderbolt. And there came upon Atlantis violent earthquakes and floods, and fire from the skies, and in a single day and night of rain all the warlike men in a body sank into the earth, and the island of Atlantis disappeared, and was sunk beneath the sea."

The Baron looked up from his book. "Plato places the island of Atlantis twelve thousand *stadia* west of the Pillars of Hercules, or Gibraltar—that would be about two thousand, seven hundred kilometres."

"In the middle of the Atlantic Ocean," I said.

"But imagine, Herr McCracken," said the Baron, "that we were to measure those twelve thousand stadia east from Gibraltar, rather than west."

Ariadne frowned. "That would put Atlantis—" She looked down at the map. Her slender forefinger traced a line from Gibraltar all the way to—

"Precisely, fräulein," said the Baron, before the rest of us really understood. "Just north of Crete: the island you all have on the map observed. Thera, the centre of the Minoan culture, that existed before ancient Greece."

"But we don't have any good reason for measuring east instead of west," I protested.

The Baron chuckled again. "Ah!" he said, "but the secret is in this word." He pointed to a place halfway down the page in his book. Jaubert looked closely at it.

"*Larger*?" he said in surprise.

"*Ja*, Herr Jaubert," replied the Baron, getting quite excited now. "In Greek, the word for *larger* is *mezon*, whereas the word for *between* is *meson*. *Fraulein, meine Herren*, let us read again Plato, and let us read it as saying that Atlantis was *between* Libya and Asia. It would place this civilization precisely there." He stabbed at the map right in the middle of the strange circular island.

25

I suppose we must still have looked unconvinced, because he went on, "Consider how advanced this Minoan civilization was, *Meine Fräulein und Herren.* They built houses three and four stories high, they had water-piping systems, they managed air-flow through their buildings to keep them warm in the winter, and cool in the summer. This was far in advance of their contemporary civilizations."

Ariadne's finely-drawn eyebrows knitted together, and she looked again at the map, and then at the Baron. "I don't get it, Helleher-Stauffen," she said. "These islands have been here for thousands of years. What's different now? Nicolas here says he's often been swimming there. So have a lot of people. What makes you think we can find Atlantis where nobody else has?"

"Not Atlantis, Fraulein Bell," chided the Baron, wagging a pudgy finger at her. "Plato called the island Atlantis because he believed it was in the Atlantic Ocean. This island was called *Thera.*"

"Sure, I understand that," said Ariadne, "but why would you want to find it anyway? I assume mere archaeology doesn't appeal to you."

The Baron gave a disdainful sniff. "Fraulein Bell," he said, "I am very interested in archaeology, but I am also a very practical man. After all, the forerunner of the archaeologist was the grave-robber, who was attracted by the promise of gold to the old burial sites."

"Gold?"

The Baron shrugged. "Not gold as such, but orichalcum."

"Ah!" declared Jaubert. "Of orichalcum I have heard, monsieur. It was a metal mined by the Atlanteans—once more, according to the philosopher Plato."

"*Sehr gut*, Herr Jaubert," said the Baron. "Please allow me, fräulein, gentlemen, once more from Plato to read." Once again he opened the book and, in his measured tones, read: "The island of Atlantis provided everything the Atlanteans needed for life. In the first place, they dug out of the earth whatever was to be found there, rock of which one was white, another black, and a third red." The Baron looked up. "Such rocks as Plato describes can be found on the island that remains, *Meine Freunde.* I have some myself, which I can show to you." He looked back at the book and read on: "They quarried many kinds of ores, and that which is now only a name, but was then something more than a name, orichalcum, was dug out of the earth in many parts of the island, being more precious in those days than anything except gold." His eyes gleamed when he looked up. "More precious than anything but gold," he repeated, as if the words were like a religious mystery to him. "Atlantis, according to Plato, was a circular island, with its capital city set at its hub. The city by concentric walls was surrounded. He describes the

27

walls as follows: 'The entire circuit of the wall, which went round the outermost zone, they covered with a coating of brass, and the circuit of the next wall they coated with tin, and the third, which encompassed the citadel, flashed with the red light of orichalcum.' Think of it, gentlemen—a whole wall plated with a metal more precious than gold! Plato goes on: 'In the city, the temple's roof was of ivory, curiously wrought everywhere with gold and silver and orichalcum; and all the other parts, the walls and pillars and floor, the Atlanteans coated with orichalcum. In the temple they placed statues of gold.' These are riches beyond imagination, *meine Freunde*!"

I noticed that Sikorsky's lip had curled. "Baron Helleher-Stauffen," he said, "is it no more than this? Riches? If you think riches is most important thing in world, then you have not read Plato closely."

The Baron was nettled once more, and stood on his dignity. "Of course there is more, Herr Sikorsky. Are you familiar with the Akashic Records?"

Sikorsky sniffed. "*Nyet*, Baron, I am not."

"The *Book of the Sky*," said the Baron, "is a Sanskrit book containing knowledge of the universe—all planes of existence, of which many are unknown to modern science. The *Book of the Sky* describes orichalcum. It says that orichalcum is a conductor of prayers. That is why it was in the temples of Thera used extensively. It gathered together the prayers of the people and channeled them."

Jaubert looked shocked. "But to whom did they pray, Monsieur Baron?" he asked.

Sikorsky and Ariadne looked a little sick too, so I tried to lighten the mood a little. "A prayer-collector?" I laughed. "Like one of those American Indian dream-catchers? Really, Baron!"

The Baron was beginning to get a permanently offended look on his face. He said, down his snub nose, "That is not all, of course. Orichalcum was also a conductor of energy, as metal electricity conducts."

"Yes?" I said, a little more interested.

"According to the *Book of the Sky*," said the Baron, "it had another name."

"Yes?"

"Its other name was *fire stone*. I believe you have a small piece of it in your pocket, Herr McCracken." He held out his hand. "Perhaps we can put the Akashic Records to the test?"

CHAPTER 3

JOURNEY ON AN AIRSHIP

We all trooped outside, clattering down the portable steps to the beaten earth of the aerodrome. The sun was low in the sky, casting a ruby hue over the airship, so that it seemed like a column of fire on its side. Last of all came Fritz. He reached into the passenger seat of the car and took out the crank handle, which he inserted and rotated a couple of times until the engine kicked into life. Then with a swift motion—almost a loving motion, I'd say, which endeared him to my heart— he had the bonnet open to expose the engine. I couldn't help stepping close to admire its beauty: shining chrome cylinder head, camshaft sprockets of gleaming brass, and excitingly dark spark plugs.

"It's a bonny piece of engineering," I commented to Fritz.

"*Ja*, Herr McCracken. *Es ist mein Kind*—she is my baby, *ja*?" He gave me a gap-toothed grin, his strange eyes lighting with pleasure.

"She's a beautiful baby, Fritz, a beautiful baby," I said, smiling.

"Fritz!" cried the Baron. "Connect the battery!"

"*Jawohl, Mein Herr!*" replied Fritz, and he took out a long electrical cable with crocodile clips at either end. One end he attached to the motor-car's battery, then touched the two wires at the other end. Sparks flew and sizzled.

Meanwhile, the Baron had set up a wooden pole in the earth, about thirty feet from the airship. At its top, the pole had a white loop, which turned out to be porcelain, when I examined it closely. The loop was in two pieces, which could be made narrower or wider by tightening or loosening a screw in the side.

"If you will place in the loop the fire stone, Herr McCracken," said the Baron. I did so, and he turned the screw a few times until the little red gem was fastened securely in the loop at the top of the pole.

People used to ask me where I got the fire stone. Well, it's simply been in my family as long as I can remember. My father gave it to me when I was a lad, and where he had it, he wouldn't tell, but I think my grandfather gave it to him. My grandfather was one of those old men your mother didn't like you to talk about—he used to smell of rum, and had a habit of singing sea shanties late at night—so naturally I asked plenty of questions about him. Apparently, he had traveled widely in his youth, picking up many strange items—the monkey's paw that was proudly displayed in our living room, for example, and the blue carbuncle shaped like a goose egg. The fire stone was shaped like a raindrop, but about an inch long. It was a deep crimson, like an ember fallen from a fire, and slightly translucent.

31

By now, the Baron had taken the electrical cable from Fritz. It sparked a little in the dimming air, and I could smell the ozone.

"You are ready, *Fraulein und Herren*?" asked the Baron with the air of a circus ringmaster. We all nodded our assent and moved in closer, but he shifted us away from the fire stone so that we were all gathered behind him. The last rays of the sun shone upon the stone, and it seemed to me that it glowed faintly, that there was even a faint shimmer of light emanating from it, like the beam of a searchlight, but reddish in hue. At the time, I just thought that a trick of the sun.

Without further preamble, the Baron touched the electrical cable to the fire stone. There came a blinding flash of light, a crashing sound like an earthquake, and a smell of ozone like sandpaper on my lungs.

For a moment, we were all blinded, and could see nothing. Then, emerging slowly from the darkness, we saw a large black crater in the red earth fifty yards away. There had been a pilots' shack there, though fortunately they had all gone home for the evening. Now, there was nothing but a few meandering trails of smoke. Some of the natives were peering at the crater with wide eyes.

"Did my fire stone do that?" I asked, amazed at the destructive power of something I had carried around in my pocket for years.

"*Ja*, Herr McCracken, *ja*. Touch it—it will not burn."

Gingerly, I touched it with my fingertips. It was completely cool. I unscrewed it and quickly transferred it to my pocket.

"Monsieur Baron, did you know the fire stone would do that?" asked Jaubert.

"I had—how is the English word?—inkling that it would." The Baron took a piece of crumpled paper from his pocket. "Here is the translation of a medieval manuscript I made some years ago. The original is a bestiary, a manuscript I discovered at the University of Aberdeen."

"Very interesting," I remarked. "I'm an Imperial College man, myself."

The Baron read his translation: "On a certain mountain, far to the east, fire-bearing stones there are which in Greek *terrobolem* are called. When by chance they draw near to each other, the fire is at once kindled, igniting everything around the mountain. But when far from each other they are, the fire within them sleeps." His eyes gleamed as he looked up at us. "Imagine what one could do with the orichalcum that we find in Thera!" he rhapsodized. "This is the ultimate power source—for everything it will provide energy: cities, armies, aeroplanes. We could to the moon fly, as the Frenchman Jules Verne has described, but using ships powered by nothing but orichalcum. We can fly around the world! We

33

can become rulers of the universe!" The Baron ceased; we were all looking at him as if he'd grown a third arm. He hastened to correct himself: "Figuratively speaking, of course."

"Potential of fire stone is easy to see, Baron," remarked Sikorsky.

"But what are we going to do to get it?" demanded Ariadne in her infuriatingly persistent way. "Dive for it? Thera is below the sea. It could take months and months to explore an underwater city, even with Nicolas' rebreathers."

"*Nein, fraulein,*" replied the Baron, and paused for dramatic emphasis. "We raise Thera!" he announced.

Ten minutes earlier, this suggestion would have been met with universal jeering. Now, we all gathered about the Baron, eager to hear his plan.

"Herr McCracken's water turbine will be more than enough to raise at least a portion of the island," said the Baron, and chuckled. He was in a good humour again.

"Baron," I said, "my water turbine was not designed to shift that volume of water. I can empty a room, but no more than that—why, I couldn't even have stopped that ocean liner from sinking last year. Raising a whole island—no, it couldn't work."

"The problem is simply one of an adequate power source and scale, Herr McCracken," said the Baron.

"I see where you're going, Baron," I said. "Yes, the fire stone could power the turbine. But it'll take time and facilities."

"My airship has a fully equipped workshop and laboratory, Herr McCracken. I think everything you need you will find on board. It will take us one week to reach the island of Thera. Will that be enough time for you?"

I looked about. Jaubert, Sikorsky, Ariadne—they had all bought into this crazy idea, and were looking at me expectantly, as if it all depended on me. Even Ariadne. Well, wasn't that a turn up for the book? Even Ariadne wanted me along by now, Rio notwithstanding.

I gave a long sigh and shook my head slowly. "I'll give it a try, Baron, I'll give it a try," I said, and there were actually cheers from the others.

"*Alles ist gut!*" declared the Baron. "Lady and gentlemen, *meine Freunde*, shall we go to the Mediterranean?"

We took off the following morning, as soon as it was light. We packed the portable steps in a special compartment on the underside of the gondola. Sikorsky stood at the controls at the front of the gondola, with Fritz at his shoulder, while Jaubert and I cast off the lines fore and aft, then scrambled up a rope ladder and in again through the door of the gondola. I strode into the *Steuerraum*, or wheelhouse, and gave Sikorsky the thumbs-up. He throttled the engines up, and the LS3 moved up and away from Marsabit.

There wasn't much for me to do, so I went aft to the *Speiseraum*. The sun shone brightly through the starboard windows, and for a while it was pleasant to watch the red earth of Kenya rolling beneath us, to watch the herds of elephants and wildebeest in the silent dust below. But after a while, a wanderlust descended on me, and I went exploring the *Luftschiff Stauffen*.

The gondola that protruded below the envelope was only half the accommodation on the airship. There was a second floor, reached by steel steps, that was constructed actually inside the envelope. The top floor contained all the cabins and bathrooms. The cabins were small, but built against the outer skin of the envelope, so that they had portholes, meaning we could always look out at the scenery, and that was wonderful. The top floor also contained a small armoury containing a rack of rifles and shotguns, and drawers of revolvers, automatic pistols, and enough rounds of ammunition to start a small war. The top deck also contained a large workshop, part laboratory, but also part metalworking and carpentry shop. Rubber-backed carpets lined the walls and ceiling so that no spark from the machinery could get into the envelope, close to the highly flammable hydrogen ballonets.

The bottom floor of the gondola consisted of the wheel-house, behind which were the navigation room, the radio room, and the galley. Then came a narrow passage, and then a small coach-house in which the Daimler was stored; the motor-car entered the coach-house by means of a ramp that could be lowered beneath the gondola. Behind the coach-house was the storage for all the food, and behind that the *Speiseraum*.

Above us, the vast area of the envelope stretched way ahead and way behind. It contained a number of ballonets, each of which was filled with hydrogen. The inside of the envelope was crisscrossed with gantries and walkways, steel lined with rubber, for the crew to perform maintenance on the ballonets and the inside of the skin, and dozens of halogen floodlights lit the area garishly. The Baron had used extra space fore and aft within the envelope for extra ballonets, and these gave the airship additional buoyancy. He had also constructed two more engines, giving the LS3 more lift and power. It could fly a little further, a little faster, with a much greater payload than its predecessors.

But soon I had to get on with my work, instead of marveling at the airship and the prospect of Africa it afforded me. Sikorsky helped me out, when Fritz took over from him at the controls, and I began to develop a friendship with the Ukrainian. Slowly, as the days progressed, four small water turbines grew in the workshop. They were heavy, but they could be carried by a single person with some effort. We needed yards and yards of hose for the pumping of the water, and Jaubert sometimes helped with them. Sometimes, Ariadne would be in there, working on her compact radio devices. The technology, she claimed, was not new; what was new was shrinking it so that it could be carried about in the hand or on the belt.

At precisely one o'clock every day, and then again at six-thirty, Fritz would call through the speaking-tube: "Herr McCracken, dinner is served in the *Speiseraum.*" And I and anybody else there would file out of the workshop, down the steps and into the *Speiseraum* in the stern of the gondola, where we usually occupied the tables with the scenic view. The conversation ranged from what we could do with the orichalcum—Sikorsky wanted to use it to power aeroplanes and airships—to the pure archaeology of finding Thera, since Ariadne had studied ancient cultures as part of her course at the University of Chicago.

It was from the panoramic windows in the LS3's *Speiseraum* that I first saw the Nile—first saw from the air, at any rate. So far, we had been flying over desert, and I had grown used to the yellow-brown for mile upon mile, when suddenly I cried out and pointed: a wide band of green dissected the yellow now. There was no fading, no part where yellow and green were mixed. The border was as sharp as a knife blade.

"*Fraulein und Herren,*" said Fritz, appearing in the *Speiseraum*, "Luxor we approach."

Leaving my dinner—an excellent filet mignon, by the way, with gently steamed lemon broccoli and rosemary scalloped potatoes—I hurried forward to the wheel-house. As the *Speiseraum*, so the wheel-house was composed almost entirely of glass. Port and starboard, the windows started at waist-height, but the for'ard windows went all the way to the deck. Fritz had taken the wheel, which looked like a ship's wheel, and his hand rested on the throttle.

I was in time to see the temple complex of Karnak, just ahead of us, a wide oblong of yellow amidst the deep green surrounding it. Dark shadows from the pillars stretched in alternating bands with the pale floor, and the temples rose like square cliffs, so high they almost brushed the underside of the gondola. A few sightseers crawled around like ants at the foot of one of the buildings.

I suddenly became aware of Ariadne standing beside me. "Beautiful," she remarked.

The evening light was soft in the wheel-house, and it outlined her profile without silhouetting her at all. "Yes, beautiful," I said, and turned again to the splendour of the past, just as it slipped below our feet and disappeared aft.

We landed shortly afterwards, amid the usual throng of squealing, delighted onlookers. Sikorsky adjusted the pitch of the engines so that the propellers were pointing upwards, and the LS3 eased down to within a few yards of the ground. Then Jaubert and I clambered down the rope ladder to secure the lines fore and aft. The engines cut, and the LS3 bobbed at her moorings. A maintenance crew approached, shouldering aside the jostling crowd, and with stepladders and a tanker began the business of refueling.

The next morning, we were off again, in the direction of Cairo. My work on the turbines went on.

Shortly after we left Cairo, I found I needed a break, and went down to the *Speiseraum* to get something to drink. Ariadne was there, staring out of the windows. We had just left the land behind us—you could see the yellow strip of Egypt to the south—and were passing over the sparkling blue plain of the Mediterranean Sea.

Ariadne turned on hearing me enter, saw that it was me, and turned back to her contemplation of the ocean.

I felt I needed to say something, so I joined her in her contemplation. After a few moments of silence, I said, "Ari, about that business in Rio."

"I know what you're going to say," she told me.

"I just wanted to say I was sorry, that's all."

"I accept your apology."

I waited for her to say something more, but nothing came. "Is that it?" I asked.

Her eyes were two pieces of ice when she turned to me. "You asked me to marry you," she said. "Then you left Rio—left the country, the continent—without any more of an apology than a scribbled note left with the concierge at my hotel." She turned back to the ocean. "Of course I forgive you," she said, "but I can't pretend it didn't happen, Mac."

"Well, never mind then," I said, gulping down my drink and slamming the glass down on the bar.

"Never mind what?" she asked, turning her cool eyes on me again. They seemed to shine now in the dim light of the *Speiseraum*.

"Never mind any of it."

"Any of what?"

"Oh, I give up!" I exclaimed, and stormed out of the *Speiseraum*.

That evening, when we were all gathered in the *Speiseraum* for supper and the Mediterranean sunset lay glittering in indigo and crimson all about us, I asked the Baron a question that had been on my mind for a while now.

"When we reach Thera," I began . . .

"Tomorrow," the Baron assured me.

"When we reach Thera tomorrow," I agreed, "what do we do? What are we looking for? I understand there's plenty of orichalcum there, but we surely can't dig it out and load it onto the LS3?"

41

The Baron shook his head, dabbing daintily at the corners of his mouth with his napkin. "A small amount is all I require, Herr McCracken. There is a place called the Lake of Fire, which I believe to contain all the raw, unprocessed orichalcum of Thera. Once we have restored the island, we can certainly whenever we wish return to retrieve orichalcum at our leisure."

I set aside my knife and fork. "Well, there are other considerations. I've nearly completed work on the portable water turbines, and I'm confident we can use them to raise a portion of the island, but not all of it—a couple of square miles would be about all. How big was Thera at its fullest extent?"

The Baron nodded. "Accounts of the size of the island vary," he said. "As for the Lake of Fire, I know roughly where it may be found."

At this point, Jaubert spoke up. "Monsieur Baron," he said, "I have been admiring your library while Messieurs McCracken and Sikorsky have worked away on these turbines. I am most impressed with your collection." The Baron inclined his head, beaming, at the compliment. "Among many books of great scholarly interest, I was able to locate a certain book by an American scholar named Edmund Elde."

Sikorsky snorted. "Scholar?" he said in derision. "The man is quack and charlatan!"

"I've seen his book on Atlantis," agreed Ariadne, "and it's the merest sensationalist garbage."

But Jaubert held up his hand. "I quite understand," he said. "Monsieur Elde's imagination was greater than his scholarship, and he speaks of Atlantis, not Thera. But notwithstanding Monsieur Elde's reputation, I find his speculations most interesting. Did you know, mademoiselle, messieurs, that the fire stone is one of several treasures to be found in Atlantis?" He waited for a response. We all looked at one another. "Elde suggested that the Atlanteans," Jaubert went on, "derived their power from the four elements—earth, air, fire, water. At each of the cardinal points at the perimeter of the island stood a temple to the Minoan deities. Each temple contained an artifact that supposedly enabled them to control one of the elements: as well as the fire stone, orichalcum, there was also a Chalice of the Tides, a Horn of Tempests, and a Globe of Earth. If a legend places these items in Atlantis, perhaps we might find them in Thera also."

There was a distinct pause before the Baron answered him. "Of these too I have heard, Herr Jaubert," he said, "but Herr Sikorsky also is correct— Elde is . . . how would you say? . . . a crank."

"He claims to speak with dead," remarked Sikorsky, "and do much with the occult. I am good Catholic. I wish to have nothing to do with his ideas."

Jaubert shrugged. "I too believe myself to be a good Catholic," he said, "and I do not wish to endorse his other beliefs, of course. But in the matter of the orichalcum he has shown himself to be accurate. It might be worth investigating."

For the moment, we dropped the conversation, and talked of other things—motor-cars and ancient manuscripts, and aeroplanes and submarines—and shortly after that, I returned to the workshop.

And the following morning, we arrived on Thera.

Chapter 4
Searching the Seabed

I'd like to tell you now about how we raised the island and immediately set about finding the vast deposits of orichalcum.

Unfortunately, it didn't happen quite like that.

The LS3 set down on Thera without a hitch, but it was late in the day and the sun was setting—a spectacle of gold and purple—so we could do nothing. Needless to say, we all arose early and barreled out of the airship without eating breakfast—Fritz was slightly annoyed.

Sikorsky had set us down on the edge of some ancient ruins, a huge complex of walls and columns, all in the sandy grey of the native rock. Sometimes, we got a glimpse of a relief or the fragment of a fresco, usually of bulls and men, sometimes with the men leaping over the bulls.

"These are astonishing," breathed Ariadne. "They're like the ruins at Knossos, the ones Sir Arthur Evans is excavating, but perhaps even better. Some people don't like the way he's restoring the buildings at Knossos, but some of these buildings are already as well preserved as his restorations."

"Pshaw!" I said. "It's all Greek to me."

"Not Greek, Herr McCracken," said the Baron—he was dressed in khaki shorts and shirt, and wore a pith helmet and dark glasses, "Minoan."

"Yes, Minoan—not Greek," said Ariadne pointedly. "The civilization that came before the Hellenic Greeks. The civilization that gave us Agamemnon and the Minotaur."

"Oh, but much more than that, Fraulein Bell," insisted the Baron. "The Minoans possessed a very sophisticated civilization—indoor plumbing, multi-story town-houses, a complex agricultural system. They managed indoor pools and skylights to cool down their houses. They even had a form of writing."

"Two forms," said Ariadne. "Linear A and B. Nobody's been able to decipher them yet."

"Not much use to have writing no one can read," I commented, but under my breath.

"And," concluded the Baron triumphantly, "they were the best warriors in the Mediterranean for centuries!"

The ruins extended ahead of us to the edge of a cliff, where they seemed to simply vanish over the edge. We stopped and stared down. Before us was the sea: deep blue in colour, with the early morning sun rippling from it like gold—or orichalcum. Immediately before our feet, the cliffs dropped away a thousand feet and more to a narrow strip of beach. On either side, the crescent arms of the island stretched away; in the middle of the bay was a low island, shaped like a shallow cone: the caldera of the volcano that had ripped the place apart, thousands of years ago.

"Somewhere out there, gentlemen, fraulein, is the lost island." The Baron took a deep breath. "Well, shall we begin?"

People have often marveled at my adventures, and told me that they would like to have a life like mine. But the odd fact is that weeks pass that are routine and uninteresting. I have occasional brushes with villains human and animal, and occasionally plants, but for the most part my life is filled with drudgery. The exciting parts tend to come at the beginning and the end of an adventure.

The first day of this adventure was filled with activity, as we flew the LS3 over to the volcanic island and then unloaded and assembled the collapsible boat the Baron stored with the Daimler in the coach-house. That was all we could achieve that day, and the following day was Sunday, so we flew to Crete to find a church where we could attend Mass. The Baron grumbled about this, since he thought it would hold up our search. But we ignored him, and resumed our business on Monday morning.

We started by loading Jaubert's equipment into the boat. It consisted of a pair of tight-fitting suits made of India rubber and large helmets with four windows like portholes. The helmet was connected

47

by a pair of tubes to a canister that contained the actual rebreather, a canister that strapped over one's shoulders.

"Jaubert, is it all right if I come down with you on the first dive?" I asked.

"But of course!" exclaimed Jaubert. "I was hoping you would ask—as the engineer, it is you who must decide where we place the turbines, *non?*"

The helmet was heavy—I felt a bit like the way a knight in the Middle Ages must have felt, putting on his great helm for a tournament. Jaubert showed Ariadne and Sikorsky how the helmet was secured, with two screws on the front and another two on the back. More India rubber sealed the helmet with the shoulder-plates. Ariadne folded her arms and looked skeptically at me. Fortunately, I couldn't hear her comments in the helmet.

The Baron took the wheel of the boat and Fritz pulled the choke so that the engine erupted into life. The boat moved away from the shore, bobbing on the waves as she moved forward. It's funny—no matter how still the water looks, small boats always toss like popcorn when they cross it.

We couldn't see the bottom of the sea after a short time, except in the vaguest way. But the water was still extraordinarily clear, and occasional flashes of light showed us where schools of fish moved through the emerald depths. And occasionally too we glimpsed something deeper—was it coral, or some type of seaweed, or was it perhaps a Doric column?

At last, Fritz turned the engine off, and the boat coasted to a halt. He tossed out the anchor and gave us the thumbs-up. Jaubert and I looked at one another. It was impossible to tell anything through the tiny portholes, but I could see the excitement in his posture. He nodded—a ponderous movement in the heavy helmet—and together we slipped over the side of the boat and into the waters of the Mediterranean.

For a few moments, all I could see in any direction was the green depths and silver bubbles racing past the portholes. Then I hit the soft sand of the seabed. The impact was only slight, but I was off-balance, and stumbled into a big bush of seaweed. For a moment I flailed around, unable to move. But then I felt something grip my arm and haul me to my feet. Jaubert had seen my plight and come to my rescue.

The first thing that struck me, on looking around, was that the underwater world was teeming with life. Life abounds in the world above the waves—trees, grass, ants, elephants—but under the sea, it surrounds you. Everywhere I looked, there was life: schools of silvery fish flitting one way and another, turtles fanning their way leisurely through the cool depths, seaweed of every colour waving and dancing. I felt as if I were in the middle of some intricate machine, its parts all moving efficiently and with infinite variety wherever I looked.

When Jaubert and I moved off, I realized that there was more to walking underwater than I had imagined there would be. I was buoyant—in spite of the lead boots and the heavy helmet and rebreather, I felt constantly as if I would float away if I didn't concentrate very hard. All the time, of course, I had to keep an eye on Jaubert, and he on me. Without any means of speaking to each other, it would have been easy to wander away and not be seen again. So we kept each other in sight as we bounded across the weird landscape, the alien underwater world.

I looked above once, and saw the narrow bullet-shape of the boat way behind us. It wouldn't do to lose sight of that either.

I began to feel thirsty, and pondered for a few moments the irony of being thirsty whilst surrounded by water. But then I noticed Jaubert stop, steady himself against the underwater eddies, and stoop. I stopped, turned, and waded over to him. He held something bright between his thumb and forefinger. As I approached, he held it out for my inspection.

It was a disc of gold, the face of a king on one side, and a bull on the other. Around the rim ran a series of strange symbols, some of which looked like tiny pictures in themselves.

We had found our first artifact.

When we got back to camp, Ariadne eagerly took the coin and vanished up the steps to the top deck. The Baron laid on some champagne, and we watched the sun go down to the popping of corks and the hooting of adventurers. Sikorsky found a sabre from somewhere—Heaven alone knows where—and like the crazy Russian he is, chopped the corks off the bottles with the blade of the sabre. It was the kind of thing he liked to do.

Ariadne joined us after a while, and sat at one of the tables in the *Speiseraum*, the coin, a notebook, and three or four dictionaries before her.

"What do you have there?" I asked.

"It's difficult to decipher," she replied. "I think it's an alphabet based on syllables, not on consonants and vowels. This symbol here and here are nominative markers, and this one a genitive marker."

"They're what?"

"The nominative means the subject of a sentence, the genitive means the possessive. The inscription probably means Someone, king of Someplace. It looks a lot like Linear B, the written language discovered by Sir Arthur Evans at Knossos." I must have looked blankly at her, for she added with a trace of irritation, "Remember, the archaeologist I told you about?"

Before I could reply, Jaubert sauntered over and handed me a glass of champagne, and we toasted the long-gone Therans. Then he said, "Mademoiselle

Bell, today McCracken and I discovered the great flaw in my diving system. We cannot communicate. Can you make radio communicators that we can install in the helmets, and allow us to talk to one another under the water?"

"I've been thinking about that," she said. "It won't be easy—radio waves go through air easier than water—but I'll see what I can do." She looked at the Baron, who had picked up the coin and was staring down at it as he turned it over and over between his fingers. "It looks like we might be onto something here," she said. The firelight caught the line of her jaw and turned her throat to gold silk. I thought we might be onto something too.

After the excitement of finding the coin, things seemed to settle down into a routine again, and we made no discoveries for a while.

"After all," the Baron said, "it is hardly reasonable that we should further discoveries expect. Thera was not simply a city, but a whole society—perhaps it is fields we explore, the countryside. We would not expect to find a large number of artifacts."

Nevertheless, it was disappointing to keep drawing a blank. It was only my work on the turbines that kept me sane during this period.

One breakthrough at this time was that Ariadne finished constructing her hand-held radio communicators. She brought them out one evening—a box with gauze at the top of it and a switch on the side.

She said, "You flip this switch up to receive a communication, and down to transmit."

"What is range?" asked Sikorsky.

"Above sea-level, about three miles," she said. "Underwater, considerably less."

"Then you have constructed them for use in the diving suits?" asked Jaubert, delighted.

But Ari shook her head. "Not yet," she said. "I'll have to build special radio communicators, with a special channel open to receive and transmit all the time."

But eventually she had them mounted in the helmets, and constructed a large and powerful radio that could be placed on the boat or in the radio room of the airship. From there, the Baron could monitor the divers, something he loved to do, grinning and chuckling and rocking back and forth as he heard them comment to one another about what they saw.

Thus it was that, when we had been two weeks exploring the emerald depths of the bay, it was my turn to listen as the divers explored the bottom. We were on the northern side of the bay, and Sikorsky and Ariadne were below. They hadn't spoken for a while, when I heard Ariadne's voice come crackling through the speaker.

"Vasili," she said, "what is that you see ahead?"

"I see nothing," replied the Russian. He sounded despondent.

More silence for a while. Then Ariadne's voice again: "There. Right ahead. That's not a natural rock formation. It looks like . . . "

For a while, nobody said anything. I had set aside my book and was sitting up straight. The sun was so bright, it was almost impossible to look at the nearby cliffs.

Sikorsky spoke again. "Now I see it, Ari!" He was excited. I called the Baron, who came hustling up from the tiny below-decks space. "What is it, you think?" asked Sikorsky.

"Well," said Ariadne, "I'm mainly a linguist, not an archaeologist, but I'd say it looks like columns and a roof."

CHAPTER 5

THE UNDERWATER TEMPLE

As the sun set that night, the tiny island across the bay cast a longer and longer shadow, like a dark finger pointing right at our boat and, just when the tip reached us, the sun disappeared and darkness descended.

And Ariadne and Sikorsky ascended.

Ariadne pulled herself into the boat, and I helped her take off the helmet and rebreather before moving on to Sikorsky.

"What did you see?" demanded the Baron at once. His glasses shone with the boat's lights. "Did you approach the ruins?"

Sikorsky threw himself into one of the wooden chairs in the stern. At a signal from the Baron, Fritz pulled the motor into life and we puttered around the caldera, back towards our camp. It would take only a few minutes to reach it.

"We got there, Helleher-Stauffen," said Ariadne, "but it was too dark to see anything. We'll have to go back tomorrow morning. But . . . " She hesitated. I could see puzzlement pressed into the soft skin between her dark eyebrows.

"But? But? What is this *but* mean?" In his excitement, the Baron had forgotten good grammar.

"Well, I can't be sure," said Ariadne slowly, "but it looked as if light was coming from behind the columns."

"But the light—it fade as we get closer, Baron," finished Sikorsky.

"*Licht!*" exclaimed the Baron. "*Gott im Himmel,* what kind of light?"

Ariadne shrugged. "Just light, Baron—a kind of greenish light. But I can't be certain of the light at all, and it might have been that colour just because everything down there looks green."

"Are you sure about what you saw?" I asked. "After all, the light's getting pretty bad down there."

Ariadne flashed a venomous look at me, but the Baron prevented her from making the inevitable acid reply. "*Wo war das?*" he demanded. Then he shook his head, as if to shake the German out of it and said, "Where was it, this column, this set of columns?"

Ariadne pointed. "Right there, against the base of the caldera."

"A doorway into volcano," said Sikorsky.

"Doesn't sound safe to me," I commented.

"Afraid, Mac?" challenged Ariadne with a sneer. Almost but not quite under her breath, she added, "Afraid of underwater temples and marriage."

"Hey, stop right there," I said. "I'll go anywhere I have to. But going inside a volcano sounds more like stupidity than courage to me."

"Mac, the volcano has been extinct for almost four thousand years!" insisted Ariadne.

"Well, all right then, I don't mind doing a bit of exploring down there. But if the thing blows up, don't blame me."

We had reached the camp now, and Fritz let out the choke and eased the boat up the beach. We piled out to tell Jaubert the news.

The following morning, we decided that Sikorsky and I would go and explore the temple—if it was a temple. Everyone assumed that's what it was, but I didn't think Ariadne had got a close enough look at it to tell anything. This morning, though, everyone went along. Nobody wanted to stay with the airship.

It was a little after nine in the morning when Sikorsky and I slipped over the side and plunged through the twilight green to the bottom of the sea.

As soon as we hit the bottom we turned in the direction of the caldera. Huge chunks of rock were piled higher and higher, with great waving fronds of underwater trees poking out here and there. I could see no temple.

"McCracken, you read?" came Sikorsky's voice through the radio.

"I read," I replied.

"Is off to right," he said.

Off we went, bounding across the floor of the sea in slow motion. We were on the northwestern side of the caldera, which meant that, early in the morning, the caldera was all in shadow. It wasn't the best time for looking for something, and I was reminded that Ariadne had found the temple, or whatever it was, in the early evening, when the dying sun's rays were slanting through the water and lighting up the whole cliff-face before her. We didn't have that advantage.

We walked and walked to the right, but I saw nothing except seaweed and schools of fish. A turtle eddied past at one point. But no temple. Nothing human.

And then I thought I could see, very dimly, a greenish light ahead of us, shining out of the face of the cliff.

"Sikorsky! Look!" I pointed.

"I see, McCracken. Let us go."

You can't really redouble your pace underwater, but we redoubled our effort. After a few yards, I was fairly sure that there really was a light.

"Ariadne, I can see the light," I said. "It's green all right, but it's still very faint."

"Apology accepted, Mac," came Ariadne's crackly voice through the radio. I grunted back at her noncommittally.

"I can make out columns on either side now," I said. "I mean, they might just be natural columns of rock. But I can see how you would think they were man-made."

Even so, as we got closer, what appeared to be a roof began to emerge from the shadows above the columns, a wide triangle with a long hypotenuse and an obtuse apex. There were two more columns, one on either side. The columns seemed to taper slightly towards the base, which was unusual. The green light seemed to be shining quite strongly, from an opening between the central columns. It had a rectangular shape, like a glowing doorway.

"Ari, I think you may have been right—I think the light is shining through an open doorway, but I can't guess what could be on the others side."

"Don't guess, you idiot," she replied. "Go and find out."

The columns were growing in front of us now. And we could see that they rose from a high platform. A flight of steps rose out of the sand to the platform. Sikorsky and I reached the steps and began to climb. Two paces only—the rest of the steps were submerged below the sand—and we stood in the doorway. Sikorsky's suit was actually lit up faintly with green from the doorway.

"Okay, Baron, Ariadne," I said, "we're at the top of the steps now and looking through the doorway. Can't see anything yet."

"Wait, Mac!" came Ariadne's voice. "If there's rock between us, you won't be able to communicate with us."

"Will we be able to communicate with each other?" I asked.

"Yes, so long as there's not too much solid matter between you."

"Then one of us will go in—just to the edge—and the other will stay here and describe what's going on. Sikorsky?"

"*Da*?"

"Do you want to go in, or shall I?"

There was a long pause.

"Boys," said Ariadne's voice, "I can't believe you can't figure this out."

"I have answer," said Sikorsky. "I go. You stay, McCracken."

"Righto," I agreed.

Sikorsky began to walk towards the doorway. The light darkened his outline, even distorted it slightly, so that he looked like some strange underwater humanoid striding through the deeps.

"He's walking towards it," I said, so the folks up top would know what was going on. "He's reached the doorway."

"*Bozhe moi!*" Sikorsky exclaimed. "My God, McCracken, it's wonderful!"

"What do you see?" I asked.

"What's he saying?" demanded Ariadne.

"He's seen something—something wonderful, he says."

"Go and see what it is," said Ariadne. "You can describe it to us when you get up top again. Ariadne out."

I strode forward, the radio signal hissing to silence as I moved closer to the temple and the roof cut us off. Sikorsky looked over his shoulder and beckoned me.

"Look, McCracken, look!"

I joined him at the threshold. Immediately before us was a sheer rock-face, up which ascended a flight of stone steps. But the top steps were dry. In fact, the surface of the water was just a few feet above our heads, and something—many somethings—shone with a green light upon the surface of the water, shattering the light into a glimmering plane of iridescence.

Sikorsky and I exchanged glances, and then started walking up the steps. Within a few moments, our heads broke the surface and water sluiced off our helmets.

We were in a huge underwater cavern. Light poured down from above, onto a forest. That's right, a forest. The cavern—and we couldn't see the edges of it—was full of lush vegetation. A thick carpet of grass stretched before us and, further off, clumps of ferns sprouted between palms and other trees. Lianas were draped back and forth through the jungle, and flowers of every colour rioted in every direction.

Nearby, on a moss-covered rock, a parrot was cleaning its bill.

We reached the top of the steps and stepped onto the soft grass. Slowly, I reached up and unscrewed the toggles on the helmet. There was a slight hiss, and I pulled it off. We drew in deep lungfuls of air. It was sweet, and smelled of damp, warm earth.

"McCracken," said Sikorsky in a hushed voice, "this is . . . wonderful. Is like flying, like good poetry, like . . . I cannot say what is like."

Slowly, we turned about on our heels. High above us, sunlight poured in through a circular hole—the vent of the extinct volcano. The light was refracted through a thousand, perhaps a million green crystals embedded in the roof of the cavern, larger than stars, and shining with a steady light. At first, I thought they were arranged haphazardly over the surface of the roof, but then I saw that they formed patterns. The one I could identify was a pair of horns and a bull's head.

"How has this lasted all this time?" I wondered. "These are not the kinds of plants that can live in a cavern."

"They have light," said Sikorsky, pointing up at the myriad green crystals. "They need also fresh water."

Slowly, we moved off through the dense undergrowth. The parrot spread its wings and flew off. A monkey nearby paused in cleaning its fur to watch us with wide eyes as we passed. We could hear the sound of birds and insects all around us, a little like the noise you hear constantly in the Amazon. And as we went on, we heard another noise, growing steadily strong—the tinkle of running water.

Sikorsky nudged my shoulder and pointed through the undergrowth. There, between the trees, we caught sight of a wall and a one of those columns that tapered towards the base, daubed with flaking red paint. We moved off towards it.

A few more paces brought us into a clearing. At the far side stood what looked like a private house or small palace of some kind. The doorway stood open, and above it was a balcony. Terracota tiles covered most of the roof, but they also lay in heaps on the ground. On either side, scarlet columns with black capitals held up what looked like cloisters, crumbling in places, overgrown with vines. In the centre of the clearing was a wide stone basin, filled with blue water, and in the middle the statue of a maiden, pouring an amphora into the basin. Water was actually pouring from the spout of the amphora. In ages past, this had evidently been the garden of a villa.

Sikorsky and I took a close look at the fountain. The colour of the water was caused by the fact that the basin was lined with copper, which had corroded to a bluish-green over the centuries.

"The Minoans," Sikorsky said, "they had running water—the Baron says so."

I dipped my hand into the water and scooped some into my mouth. It was sweet. "Well," I said, "now we know they had fresh water."

Together, we walked through the garden towards the villa. It was considerably darker inside, but as our eyes got used to the darkness, we saw pillars on either side, and frescoes on the walls that depicted dolphins, octopi, and other sea creatures. Passing through this chamber to the next one, we paused to take stock.

Against the further wall were steps leading up to the next story, but between us and the steps was another pool. In the middle of the pool stood a strange contraption, gears and wheels and pulleys, perhaps twenty feet in height.

A pair of windows in each wall lit the chamber up. Pulling myself away from the mechanical wonder, I went over to one of the windows and looked out. Through the trees, I could see that the forest continued for some distance, but between the trees rose a massive column of rock, several miles away. The rocky column rose to a plateau, just below the vent of the volcano. That flat area would effectively screen what was below it from any observer staring into the volcano's mouth from outside. We were looking at what nobody had seen for four thousand years.

I breathed out heavily, and Sikorsky and I sat down on the window sill. I contemplated the utterly inscrutable machinery of the contraption that stood in the centre of the pool for a few moments.

"Ariadne's never going to believe this," I said.

CHAPTER 6
THE EXPLORATION BEGINS

I don't believe this," said Ariadne.

We were all back in the *Speiseraum* of the LS3. The twilight was growing all around: long shadows lay across the island, the sea was as dark as any wine Homer could have imagined.

"Why not?" I asked. "We were there. It's true."

"That's not what I mean," she replied. "I believe Vasili, so I believe you too. But I've never heard of anything like this before."

"It's simple," I said, and started to explain—for perhaps the sixth or seventh time. "It's a gigantic cavern, beneath the volcano we've set down next to, beneath this whole island. The cavern is immense— far bigger than the island that's above it. Within the cavern is a forest—the kind of trees and bushes and flowers and birds and beasts that you'd find in a jungle, like the Amazon. You remember the Amazon, Ari?" She frowned at me, and I went on: "There's light in there, coming through green crystals the Therans embedded in the cavern roof. And we found a villa, with an indoor pool, just like the Baron described, and a machine of some kind. I don't know what it does yet."

"It was big, very big," Sikorsky added. "We walk one mile, maybe two mile through forest, and still we are no more than halfway to plateau."

"In the centre of the cavern stands this plateau, *ja?*" said the Baron. Sikorsky nodded. "Can we on the plateau land our *luftschiff?*"

"Is difficult to say," replied Sikorsky. "Vent of volcano is perhaps too small for airship to fit, maybe not. Tomorrow, I measure."

Jaubert was doing arithmetic in his head. "This cavern," he said, "it is eight or ten miles in diameter. And a forest, it stands in the cavern, no?"

"That's correct," I said.

"Sunlight the trees obtain from these crystals, through which light from outside is refracted, *oui?*" I nodded. "The trees, they need sunlight for—how you say?—*photosynthèse.*"

"Photosynthesis," I suggested.

"*Oui, naturellement*—photosynthesis. But the forest you describe, monsieur—it is more than light it needs to survive. It needs also water. Not the sea, but . . . ah . . . *de l'eau douce.* I cannot say what is *eau douce* in English."

"Sweet water . . . fresh water!" said Ariadne. "Of course, all those plants would need fresh water, and so would the animals."

"The fountain in the garden and the pool in the house contained fresh water," I said. "I tasted both, and there was no trace of salt in it."

"Ha!" declared the Baron. "The Minoans—the method for the pumping of water into the houses they invented. It is by historians and archaeologists well documented."

"Then there must be a source of fresh water somewhere, and the pumps still working. After four thousand years!" As an engineer, I was frankly impressed.

"Tomorrow we can begin the explorations," said the Baron, chuckling and rubbing his fat hands together. "The water turbines will we need no longer, Herr McCracken!"

"*C'est merveilleux!*" declared Jaubert. "It is on foot we can explore with the greatest of ease."

I got up from the table and wandered over to the window that looked west. The volcano was still outlined faintly by the very last rays of the long-invisible sun, and an array of stars shone like light-dust overhead. There wasn't much of it to see because the airship's envelope loomed overhead.

After a moment, I felt a hand on my shoulder. Turning, I was surprised to see that Ari had joined me.

"It's too bad we won't be using the turbines," she said.

I shook the sentimentality out of myself. "No, it's much easier this way. Though I confess, I was looking forward to seeing if I could raise a whole island. We'll be needing your radio communicators, though."

Ariadne frowned. "That's what I was afraid of. I don't know how well they'll work down there. If there are a lot of physical obstructions, the radio waves will be disrupted."

The sun had truly gone down now, and the shape of the volcano was only a darker shape against the dark, star-bespeckled sky. I knew we would rise early the following morning, so I turned in without saying goodnight to anyone but Ari.

The next morning, we did indeed rise early. Sikorsky strode off up the side of the volcano, carrying a theodolite in a wooden case, to measure the vent, and Jaubert went with him. I couldn't find the Baron anywhere, though the door of the library was locked, so I guessed he was in there, reading, as was often his habit. I could only find Ari.

"I think we should go and map what we can of the underwater Thera," I suggested.

To my surprise, she agreed readily. "I'd like to try out the radios in the environment down there," she said.

We spent about an hour packing for the trip. Jaubert had brought a waterproof chest, large enough to contain a pair of backpacks, which we packed carefully.

"Ski poles?" said Ari, holding one up and examining it skeptically.

"Useful when you're trekking through the wilderness—they help you over uneven ground. Better than an alpenstock."

"It would have to be a bit longer."

I took it from her and showed how the bottom half fitted inside the top half and could slide out to any length. "Clever, isn't it?" I said. "Solid steel—it'll never break!"

"You built it, didn't you?"

I smiled, and she stuffed a pair into each backpack.

"Did you pack the mirrors?" she asked.

"Do you think we'll need them?"

"Useful for signaling, if we need to."

"There's no sun down there."

"Just in case." She sat back on her haunches. "Okay, now, we each have a first-aid kit, a revolver and spare ammunition, rope, a ball of twine, food, radio, water bottles, a light jacket each. Anything else?"

"I think we have all we need," I said, pushing my toolbox in—it contained the basic tools I needed in most situations, along with a basic set of wheels, gears, and pulleys. You never know when you'll need them.

"Good. Then let's go." She closed and locked the chest and we carried it between us to the boat.

We took the boat out to the far side of the island, dropped anchor, and slipped the diving suits over our outdoor clothes. Ari dropped the chest over the side, paying out line slowly so that it wouldn't get lost or damaged. Then we helped each other fasten the helmets and rebreathers on and slipped over the side. We had learned that the best way to dive was to climb over the side of the boat and hold onto the side until we could release ourselves gently, and this we now did, sinking through the green waters to the bottom, which we hit with a gentle impact.

We found the entrance to the cavern without any difficulty, and soon emerged, dripping, into the jungle. The green light twinkled down on us from the roof of the cave as Ari twisted the screws on her helmet and wrenched it from her head. She stood slack-jawed and—what must have been difficult for her—silent as she gazed, awe-struck, at the trees, the birds, the flowers, the light.

"I've never seen anything like this," she finally admitted breathlessly. "It's more wonderful than I imagined."

We opened the chest and took out the radios and backpacks, then folded the diving suits as neatly as we could and put them inside, with the rebreathers. Shouldering the backpacks, we struck out through the forest, following where my memory took us, towards the house with the pool. Ari walked as if she were in a dream, saying nothing but occasionally pointing when she saw a huge butterfly go bobbing across our path or a jeweled bird sitting

71

in a tree. Once, a snake slithered through the under-growth beside the path. It was black and white and hooded like a cobra, so we remained perfectly still until it had slithered away.

When we had been walking for about thirty minutes, we found the villa. Ari stood wordlessly on the threshold of the garden. After a few moments, she walked over to the cloister and examined one of the columns closely. Looking at me, she said in a quiet voice, "The paint looks original. Four thousand years old. I can hardly believe it."

"It's a bit flaky," I said. "I think it needs a new coat."

She punched me on the arm.

"Come and look at this," I urged her, steering her through the garden and into the house. She stood for a few moments admiring the frescoes, but I moved her along into the room beyond. "There," I said, pointing to the large machine in the pool. "Isn't she a beauty?" We started walking slowly around the perimeter of the pool. The contraption consisted in the main of two huge bevel-gears, one horizontal and at the top of a huge shaft, the other on its side so that the rotation of the one would cause the rotation of the other. For the rest, it was a wonderful mass of pulleys, crank-shafts and gears, all gleaming orichalcum. "It's sublime!" I enthused.

"Sublime?" echoed Ari.

"Yes, sublime," I said, pointing. "Look at that. See how ideally proportioned those pulleys are on the front of that shaft? Look at how stately the column is that holds the vertical bevel-gear—it looks like a queen, holding the gear, with love."

"That's quite an imagination you have," remarked Ari.

"No, no, it's all there, it's really there." I pointed again. "See the wheel at the bottom—we call it a Persian Wheel now. It's used in the East to irrigate fields. Here it scoops up water and deposits it on that chain-pump pump. The water from the chain-pump pump drives the wheel on the front of that shaft, which transfers energy by all those pulleys up to the bevel-gear. I tell you, it's perfect. It's not just engineering—it's a work of art!"

"You'd see perfection in a shoe factory," said Ari.

"No, I wouldn't," I retorted. "No, I don't. See, the humanity's been taken out of the factory—but this expresses humanity, the humanity of the engineer who designed it, thousands of years ago. This is a man who saw God and depicted Him in cogs and wheels and proportion and material and motion. A factory has no soul. There's nothing divine in it. But this has soul and divinity—an evil mind could not have designed this. I wish I could see it work."

"What is it?" Ari asked.

"I haven't the faintest idea," I replied. "Beautiful, though, isn't it? Don't touch it!" She had been reaching out towards one of the levers. "We don't know what it will do," I explained.

Ari, unable to comprehend the ineffable beauty of the whatever-it-was, wandered over to the window and surveyed the forest beyond the house, the plateau at the top of the rock column, the gem-strewn roof beyond it. From here, you could see that the gems formed a picture of a bull with a man leaping over its back.

Ari turned about, businesslike now. "Shall we test the radios now?" she suggested. I nodded my agreement, pulling myself with reluctance away from the mechanism. "The heavy forest here will be a good test of the radio waves," she explained.

I took the radio she held out to me. "You stay here," I said, "and I'll step out into the garden—let's see how the radios work at different distances."

I strode out through the next room and into the garden, standing beside the fountain. I pressed the transmit button on the radio. "Are you there, Ari?" I asked.

"I'm here," she said. "The signal's strong."

"I'm going on." A dozen steps beyond the gate, and I was in the deep forest beyond the perimeter of the garden. "How about now?"

"There's a little distortion. How far away are you?"

I looked over my shoulder. From here, I couldn't see the garden or the house, but I knew how many paces I had come. "About fifty yards," I said.

"Go another fifty."

I walked a little further. The forest seemed to be thinning a little, and ahead I thought I could see a more open area of land. "Ari," I said, "the land seems to be changing—there aren't trees ahead."

"I hear you," she said. "Keep going."

Between the trees, I saw strings of mist rising from the ground. It was a yellowish mist, and there was a faint smell of sulphur on the air.

"Mac, can you hear me?" came Ari's voice through the radio.

"I can hear you," I replied. "I seem to be emerging from the forest—there's flat land ahead, and a kind of yellow mist. And the ground seems a lot softer."

"Don't go any further," said Ari. "The signal's strong. Let's go on together."

I stopped, looking out into what appeared to be a marsh. Before me, bending over the edge of some water, was what appeared to be an elephant, about the size of a Newfoundland dog. Setting the radio on a rotten tree-stump, I advanced cautiously into the marsh.

The elephant was drinking the water greedily. I could hear the slurpings and gluggings. At one point, it looked up and burped.

75

"I think I'll call you Ariadne," I said.

Amazingly enough, I realized as I watched it that I was looking not at a young elephant, but a full-grown pygmy elephant, the kind of beast that had been extinct for thousands of years.

"Mac, Mac, are you there?" came Ari's voice from the radio.

A little reluctantly, I turned away from the beast-ie towards the radio.

But I found I couldn't move.

While I had been watching the elephant, I had sunk past my ankles in quicksand, and now I couldn't budge my feet an inch.

CHAPTER 7
THE ISLAND MOVES

My first thought on finding my feet stuck—and sinking!—was of a Sherlock Holmes book I had read recently, in which the murderer had died because he had run through a swamp and fallen into quicksand.

I made an effort to pull my feet up out of the mud, but they wouldn't move. I tried again, and again, with rising trepidation, but found myself at the end of my efforts stuck as fast as ever, and even a little deeper in the muck. I struggled to free my feet, but could move neither backwards nor forwards, to the left nor to the right.

The elephant watched me, and evidently satisfied with the water she had drunk, ambled away without a care in the world. I had named her aptly, I thought.

Fear grew in me, and I renewed my efforts with an energy only desperation could have given me. But it was no good. I couldn't move an inch. The soft, clingy sand was halfway up my shins.

"Mac, Mac, come in!" came the tinny voice of Ariadne. I looked up sharply. The radio had fallen off the tree-stump and into a low bush. I reached out, strained, struggled—it was at least a foot and a half beyond my reach. I tried to move my feet, but I could not feel the bottom, and I sank further. "God!" I cried out, making the Sign of the Cross quickly. "I could use a little help, here!"

"Mac, where are you?" It was Ariadne, not God. "Please respond!"

"I will, Ari," I said out loud, my teeth gritted, "just as soon as I can reach that wretched button!"

I reached out again and, again, sank further. I was up to my knees by now.

Maybe if I'm perfectly still, I thought, I'll float to the top of the quicksand.

I tried it. Three of four seconds crawled past. The quicksand crept a tiny bit up past my knees.

A sound came from the forest, like a large animal crunching through the undergrowth. I looked up, my eyes wide. The sound came again. I plunged my hand under the surface of the quicksand in an attempt to reach my boot-knife, but I couldn't get it out of the sheath amidst all the slime.

The trees rustled again, and Ariadne emerged from them.

"Thank God!" I cried. "Help me, please!"

"Mac," she said in an urgent voice, "where is the radio?"

"What? I dropped it. Can you please—"

"You dropped it!" She peered into the quicksand. "Do you think you can reach it?" she asked.

I stared at her for a gob-smacked moment. "No," I said, "it's a little beyond my reach. Ariadne, will you please help me?"

"I must know where the radio is," said Ariadne. "It's a very important piece of equipment."

"Yes, so am I," I answered. "Ariadne, I'm sinking!"

"Oh, stop whining," she told me. "I need to get the radio back. Can you dive for it, please?"

"It's not in the quicksand," I said. "I am." A noxious bubble escaped from deep down in the quicksand, and I slipped a little further under it. It was nearly up to my waist.

Ariadne looked relieved. "Then where is it?" she asked.

I pointed. "There! There! Now will you please help me out of this?"

She looked around. "Where?"

"Help me out and I'll show you," I said, from between gritted teeth.

She looked at me, her head cocked on one side, and for the first time, it seemed, noticed my danger. "I left my backpack in the villa," she explained, "but you have some rope in your backpack too. Can you reach it?"

"Hmm, let me think . . . No, my movements are a little restricted right now, Ari. You might have to reach in and pull me out."

"This is a silly predicament you've gotten yourself into," observed Ari. "This is what happens when you go wandering off by yourself."

"Ari, I'll let you nag me like you're my Mum when I'm out of this quicksand and on dry land. But can you please in the meantime do something other than talk?"

Clicking her tongue and shaking her head, Ari reached out and took me by the scruff of the neck. She pulled hard. I fell over backwards onto the sand, yelling out in dismay and outrage.

But I found that I hadn't sunk. I was lying flat on the surface of the quicksand. Falling over backwards had broken the seal around my legs, which had thus been freed.

"Now do a slow back-stroke, and you'll get to the shore in no time," Ari instructed me.

I tried it. It worked. She reached down, and pulled me onto firm ground. I stood dripping before her, and she started to laugh.

"I don't see what's so funny," I said, attempting to recover my dignity and failing. "There's your blasted radio." I pointed.

"Oh, don't be such a self-important buffoon," she said, and kissed me on the nose quickly before picking up the radio and heading off through the forest back towards the villa. I was so surprised that I stood gaping for a full minute before following her.

I found her beside the pool, that beautiful contraption towering over her. She had a screwdriver out and was tightening something or adjusting something else on the radio.

"Why did you do that?" I asked.

"What?"

"Why did you kiss me?"

"I was glad to see you safe," she replied. She looked up from her work at me, her lips pursed and her eyes narrowed. "Really, you do make a fuss."

"Well, it was a bit unexpected—I'd have been a lot less surprised if you'd slipped a dagger between my ribs."

"Well, after what you did to me—"

"Oh, here we go again!"

"What?" She stood up and thrust her hands on her hips. "What do you mean, *Here we go again*?"

"What I mean," I said, stepping closer to her and speaking directly into her perfect face, "is that you always want to drag up the past."

"It's the only thing I have to judge you by."

"But it makes me look bad!"

"Maybe you *are* bad."

"Maybe you're exaggerating—where are you going?"

Ariadne spun round from the doorway. "Into that marsh," she said. "Weren't we here to explore and map?"

"All right, then. I'll see you later," I said, stooping over my backpack and adjusting the straps and buckles.

Ariadne didn't move. "You know," she said, "you were never in any danger. Don't you remember what Felipe told us when we were on the Amazon?"

"Who?

"Felipe, our guide. He told us about quicksand. He told us all you need to do is lean forward and swim slowly. Nobody ever dies in quicksand, except in Sherlock Holmes novels. Nobody who knows how to cope with it, anyway." She paused a moment, watching me as I took out one of Fritz's sandwiches and chomped on it. "Do you remember that, or were you too busy messing with the outboard motor?"

"I thought I could get it to go faster," I said. "But, by the way, that's exactly what I was talking about."

"What do you mean?" she asked.

"It's what I was talking about in Rio. I'm in danger like that all the time. I can't expect a wife and children to have to face the prospect of possibly losing me in the kind of circumstances I confront every day."

Ariadne didn't say anything, and when I looked up at her, I saw that her lips were pressed tightly together. "I was willing to face all those dangers with you," she said. "You didn't let me choose—you just ran away. And what does it matter anyway? Whatever God has planned for us is right. Now are you coming with me, or would you prefer to stay here with your silly machine?"

I snorted a laugh out. "At least the machine doesn't talk nonsense," I replied, turning to reach for my backpack. But I never got it. I felt a shove on my back, and went sprawling into the fountain. I flailed around for a bit, and then reached out and clutched something to lever myself up.

It moved in my hand.

"What have you done?" wondered Ari.

"I don't know," I said, pulling myself out of the pool.

Over our heads, a series of little vents in the wall near the ceiling of the villa had opened, and water poured out of them. The Persian Wheel began to move. Up went its arms, each one scooping up water and then throwing it onto the chain-pump pump. The chain-pump pump moved, sluggishly at first, but then with greater purpose. The pulleys started to rotate. With a grinding sound, the huge bevel-gears started to turn around, faster and faster as more water poured down into the pool. The chain-pump on the upright bevel-gear started to clank as the teeth of the inner gear slotted into its links and dragged it around. From down below our feet came the screech of gears and pulleys, unseen and long unused, slowly grinding into action. The ground throbbed. Ripples bounced across the water in the pool. Over our heads came a great cracking noise, like rocks breaking. Ariadne pointed.

"Mac—look at the cavern roof!" The gems that distributed light throughout the cavern were shaking, and it seemed that lines of blue light, running from the horizon to the volcano's vent, had appeared. "What's happening?"

I looked at the lever I had pulled, and felt a little queasy. "I don't know," I answered. "I wonder if I did that." The lines of light were wider now, and widest of all at the top, near the vent. "Part of me wants to find out," I said, "part of me wants to stay and watch this."

"That's not the intelligent part of you," Ariadne replied. "I don't know what's happening here, but I bet we're safer on the seabed. Come on!"

We made a dash for it. All around us, the trees were quivering. Parrots and other birds, startled by the motion and the unaccustomed noise, had scattered into the air, and the undergrowth rustled with startled creatures, dashing like us, but without knowing where. The ground trembled under our feet.

We reached the steps by which we had entered the cavern earlier, and took our suits out of the chest. But we didn't put them on at once. I was looking at the cavern roof. The blue lines we had seen earlier were much wider by this time, and splayed towards the apex of the roof. The blue light was actually the sky—I could see clouds now—and the roof had divided into sections, each like the blade of a knife, which would all fit together in a dome. The green gems still shone, but faintly compared with the dazzling Mediterranean sky.

"Did we do all this?" Ari wondered.

"It's the most spectacular piece of engineering I've ever seen," I said in wonderment.

"Are we safe here?" Ari asked.

I couldn't answer. By now, the roof sections were upright, like a circle of knives pointing towards the sun. A new sound broke out: more gears, wheels, cogs, pulleys, somewhere underground. The knife blades began to shrink into the ground. As they retracted, I could see more of the world beyond, and I saw that the whole island was rotating and rising, as if on a giant screw-thread.

Ari tugged at my sleeve and pointed. A dark shape stood out against the sky, like a pencil or cigar. It was getting closer and closer. Something detached from the bottom of the shape and unfurled towards us. It was a rope ladder. Ariadne and I exchanged glances.

"You go first," I said, and as she began to haul herself up towards the LS3 I hastily packed the diving suits back into the chest. I hooked it to the bottom rung of the rope ladder and began my own ascent towards the gondola. The round face of the

85

Baron, his eyes obscured by his spectacles, was framed by the doorway. He urged me on with motions and words I couldn't understand. Ari was already in the gondola, and now she reached down to me. In a moment, I was at her side. Together, we hauled up the rope ladder and the chest, then the Baron slammed the door closed.

We all peered through the porthole in the door at what was outside.

What was outside was hard to describe. It was a great circular island in the middle of the sea, vast in area, a great column of rock rising from its middle, like the axle of an overturned wheel. It was slowly rotating and rising from the waters. The roof of the cavern had been man-made. It had been constructed by those ancient workmen in sections, and those sections protected the island against the sea when it was submerged; the island rising once more from the waters, the roof retracted, as we had witnessed. And now that the roof was gone, we could see that the whole island was bounded by a wall—I blinked a few times, because I could hardly believe my eyes—of a shining, reddish substance. We had found orichalcum.

But there was more. The island we had walked on was only the inner circle of a number of concentric rings, and now the roof was rising off an outer ring, revealing more forest, more marshes, lagoons, cliffs. It went on for miles and miles and miles—beyond sight.

The LS3 leaned over a little, and I could tell that we were altering our course. Ariadne and I dashed for'ard to the wheel-house, the Baron puffing behind us. Sikorsky was at the controls, Jaubert and Fritz on either side of him, staring in wonder out of the for'ard windows. Sikorsky looked over his shoulder and gave a wild laugh.

"Call me fool," he said, "but I will land there—at top of mountain."

"That's folly all right," I said. "Can't you wait until the island has stopped moving?"

The Russian's only reply was another wild laugh. He pushed on the wheel and the airship slid down towards the plateau.

"McCracken," said Sikorsky, "you and Jaubert jump and secure dirigible."

"Right you are," I said. Jaubert and I dashed from the wheel-house, past the radio room and into the passageway.

"I'll release the lines," came Ariadne's voice.

I nodded and pushed open the door. Immediately, a blast of warm air from outside buffeted our faces. The wide disc of the plateau—we later called it Russian Folly—lay below us, the ground closing slowly. It was a barren top, with nothing growing on it at all, just pale sand and a scattering of rocks that looked like a series of low walls.

Jaubert had unhitched the trunk from the rope ladder, so I kicked the ladder out and swung myself down. Jaubert followed. In a few moments, we were on the ground. The fore lines hung from the underbelly of the LS3, like a pair of spindly legs. I took one, Jaubert the other, and we secured them to fragments of masonry. Then we dashed aft to catch the next pair of lines. Inside the gondola, Ariadne turned the crank, hauling the lines in, and the LS3 descended until the gondola was some six feet above the ground. Her silhouette appeared for a moment in the doorway, and then she leaped down, without bothering to use the rope ladder. She joined me and Jaubert on the edge of Russian's Folly as we looked down at the new island.

To the south lay the tops of trees, undulating with the ground below. Through it, and aiming mostly southwards, threaded a silver river. The villa we had found lay almost due west. North were marshes, the sun shining on wide expanses of water, the yellow mist hanging low in the crevices. Beyond it, just emerging from the sea, rose mile after mile of land—low hills nearby, but green plains further out, and stretching even to the horizon. I could see forests, cliffs, deserts, towers, palaces, roads, castles, farms. Thera was immense—three concentric rings, each bounded by a wall.

The island stretched nearly out of sight. From our elevation, we could see a distant glimmer of water that marked the outermost boundary of Thera, something like twenty-five miles away.

"Nobody's ever going to believe this," said Ari.

CHAPTER 8
THE TEMPLE OF THE MINOTAUR

The next morning we began exploring the continent of Thera from the air. We took off from the Folly and started, first of all, to fly in a tight circle around the tall column of rock. We saw that, threading up its side, was a long series of stone steps. The steps wound about the pillar of rock three times before reaching the plateau on top and, as we saw it from the air, I became more and more convinced that on the Folly had once stood the royal palace of Thera. The open space in which we had moored the LS3 was a central courtyard, around which were mazes of buildings. Some of the chambers on the north side were large, and looked like public spaces—throne rooms, feasting halls, and one wide staircase leading to an upper hall that was quite well preserved. The rooms on the south side were smaller, and probably private quarters for the king and his household. To the east was a cobbled space with the remains of two lines of pillars—possibly a forum. To the west was a semi-circular space surrounded by stepped seating that looked a lot like a theatre.

Ariadne, who had some interest in the ancient world since her days at the University of Chicago, and could read Greek and Latin and a number of other languages I'd never heard of, seemed more interested in speculating about the Minoan language.

"The Minoans had no real alphabet," she explained to me on that first day, as I was staring out of the window, attempting to chart the ground below, "at least, not an alphabet as we'd understand it. They carved hieroglyphs into stone. Do you know what hieroglyphs are?" She paused long enough to hear my grunt of acknowledgement. "They're pictures that represent words or concepts. As a result, we don't know a lot about their language."

To port, a silver ribbon of water erupted from the base of the rock column and wove through the jungle. Immediately below us, the ground rose, and the river cut through a gorge. I could see a bridge spanning the gorge, gleaming like copper in the early morning sun. I was trying to estimate how far from the foot of Russian's Folly the bridge was, and wishing I could take a couple of years to survey and map the whole place.

"There are a few very late inscriptions in a Minoan language called Eteocretan," Ariadne went on, "and the curious thing is that the language is not related to Greek or Latin or any other Indo-European language."

The river, I saw, flowed mainly southwards, though I could see it bend west a little off to starboard. As the airship moved, it dwindled with distance.

"It's possible that Eteocretan is related to the Philistine languages. You remember them from the Old Testament, of course."

"That's very nice," I said, moving to another window to get a last glimpse of the river. Was it saltwater or fresh? I wondered.

"It's perhaps similar to the Etruscan language spoken in Italy before the arrival of the Latins. You remember the story Vergil tells in *The Aeneid*?"

"Fondly," I replied. The river was slipping from sight.

"You remember how the Trojans befriend the Etruscans? Well, they perhaps spoke a language similar to the Minoans, which is therefore similar to the one spoken by the Therans."

"Mm-hm," I said, moving to another window as the river disappeared behind us, and adding a few lines to my sketch.

"And of course the Minoan language is related to Middle Ancient Gibberish," said Ariadne. "That was established by Doctor Monkey-Brain in the late Jurassic period."

"I knew it," I muttered, hastily erasing some of my sketch and re-drawing some of the lines.

I became aware that a long silence had drawn out between us, and looked up at Ariadne.

"You haven't been listening to a word I've said," she observed.

I cleared my throat. "Certainly I've been listening intently. The Therans spoke a language called Hieroglyphic, and they talked to one another about monkeys." I paused, thinking hard about what I'd just said. "Or something like that," I added.

"You're just not interested in their language," Ariadne said bitterly, and left the *Speiseraum*.

I paused for a while after she left, wondering why she was in such a snit. But then I realized that I was missing a lot of the landscape below, and returned to my sketch.

To the north of the Folly was a wide expanse of marshland. Another stream emerged from the Folly to water it, feeding a large lake that stretched east and west to within a quarter-mile of the orichalcum wall. The lake was shaped like a leaping salmon, if you used your imagination a bit. Jaubert joined me as we were flying over the lake.

"It is fascinating, no?" he said. "When we start the exploring, I say we begin here."

The next day, we explored the circle outside the orichalcum wall. It was bounded by a wall that looked as if it were plated with gold, with gates to north and south. Between the walls of orichalcum and of gold, the space was mostly water, with two large islands to west and east; these were the islands that were still visible when Thera was submerged, and the ruins on those islands seemed to be the remains of the capital city of Thera. Now the water level had dropped, the islands had tall cliffs descending to wide beaches. To the south lay a kind of barren plain, except that it was water-logged a lot of the time.

"Interesting," observed Ariadne, peering over my shoulder at it. "I can't tell if it's a desert or another marsh."

It was the third or fourth time we had passed over it, and I had seen it under very different conditions. "It's like a beach," I said, "which is sometimes covered by tidal waters, like an extension of this whole inland sea."

"What's that?" she wondered, jabbing her finger out of the window.

What appeared to be a square dune rose out of the watery sands ahead of us. On its top were rocks and spiky grass, and even a few palm trees, but we could see windows in the sides, and a wide doorway, flanked by tall columns. The columns were painted red, while the capitals were daubed with black and the walls the natural colour of the stone.

"It looks a little like the Library of Congress in Washington DC," observed Ariadne. "A different colour, though." We watched the building as it came close and then disappeared under the gondola. "That's where I'll go," Ariadne decided.

When we gathered together in the *Speiseraum* on the third evening of our aerial reconnaissance, the subject for debate was where we should begin our exploration on foot. Jaubert and Ariadne had their own ideas.

"We haven't charted all of the island yet," I said. "It would be premature to make a decision now, before we've explored the other circles."

"Tomorrow," suggested Sikorsky, "we fly due west, until we reach perimeter. Then we fly along perimeter. We work inward, not outward."

"That seems like a good idea," I agreed. "Don't you have a good idea about where we should start?"

"*Nyet*," replied Sikorsky. "Is best we split up in any case—we cover more ground that way. Ariadne can begin in library, Nicolas in lake. For me, I stay in dirigible, and fly in for rescue if things get tough, *da*?"

"*Da*," I agreed; and we had a plan.

It was five o'clock the next morning when Fritz's voice crackled through the speaking-tube: "*Fraulein und Herren*," he said, "breakfast in the *Speiseraum* awaits you." There was a clattering of feet along the corridors and down the steps, and we all assembled in the *Speiseraum* for bacon and eggs, with toast and marmalade on the side and some very welcome kippers.

"Fritz," I said, "can you make porridge?"

"Paritch?" said Fritz, a little confused. He was pouring coffee for Jaubert.

"*Haferbrei*," said Ariadne.

"*Ach! Haferbrei! Jawohl, Herr McCracken!* I make it for you tomorrow. *Mit Zucker?*"

"Under no circumstances!" I replied. "I'll have it the man's way—with salt."

"*Haferbrei mit Salz*," said Fritz to himself, pouring now for Ariadne.

"I'll take honey with mine, Fritz," said Ariadne. "You know, Samuel Johnson defined oatmeal as 'a grain, which in England is generally given to horses, but in Scotland supports the people.'"

Everybody laughed at this, except me. I said, "Well, you tell that Johnson fellow from me—"

"Fritz!" barked the Baron. "*Mein Kaffee!*" Fritz had almost finished pouring for Ariadne, and the Baron put an urgent edge into his voice: "Now, Fritz!"

"*Jawohl, Mein Herr!*" said Fritz, spilling the coffee into Ariadne's saucer and hurrying to the Baron's side. The Baron snapped at Fritz, cuffing him over the back of the head. Fritz said something apologetic to the Baron in German, bobbing up and down and wringing his hands.

"Think nothing of it, Fritz," said the Baron. He pointed to his empty cup. "Pour."

Ariadne was looking at the Baron with narrowed eyes, and there was a moment of awkward silence before she said, "The radios are working well, and I've given them a larger power source, which means we'll be able to communicate, but only within certain limits—about five miles."

"I will fly around island," volunteered Sikorsky. "At regular intervals, you all can speak with me in dirigible."

"How long will it take you to fly around the island?" I asked.

Sikorsky spread his hands. "Two hour, perhaps three."

"It is well," said Jaubert. "You are within range of communication every two or three hours. *Très bien.*"

As we filed out of the *Speiseraum*, I patted Fritz on the shoulder. "That was a grand breakfast, Fritz," I said. "You are a great cook."

"*Danke*, Herr McCracken, *danke!*" said Fritz, grinning shyly and bobbing up and down with gratitude.

Half an hour later, we cast off and the airship moved slowly, almost ponderously, into the north. The Folly dropped astern, as we passed quickly over the marsh. The yellow fog still rose from it, but it was interspersed with wide, flat lakes, shining in the morning sun. In less than two minutes, Sikorsky pulled back on the throttle. The hum of the engines dropped almost below hearing, and the airship slowed to a crawl.

"*Au revoir!*" cried Jaubert cheerfully, and disappeared through the hatch. A few moments later, we saw him jump off the bottom rung of the rope ladder, and hauled it back in.

"Monsieur Sikorsky," came the crackling sound of Jaubert's voice through the radio, "can you hear me?"

"Is very clear," replied Sikorsky (the radio had been moved from the radio room into the wheel-house). "*Do svidanya!*" He pulled on the throttle, tossed the wheel about, and brought the airship in a wide arc towards the south.

Ariadne entered the wheel-house and stood beside me. She had already donned her diving suit and rebreather, and it looked good on her. For a few moments, as we watched the land pass beneath and Russian's Folly slipping by to the port, my mind went back to the time we had spent together in Rio and along the Amazon. What a long time ago *that* was!

"Ari," I said, "I'm sorry I wasn't listening to you the other day."

"Oh," she said carelessly, "when was that?"

"You know," I replied, "when you were talking about . . . well, I don't know. I wasn't listening."

She gave a quick shrug. "I forgive you," she said. "Is that all?"

"Is that all?" I retorted. "What are you, my confessor?"

Sikorsky turned his head towards us. "Miss Bell," he said, "we approach library building."

"Thanks, Vasili," replied Ari, smiling. She turned and left the wheel-house as Sikorsky adjusted the flaps and brought the airship closer to the ground. I followed after her.

"If you mean I'm sorry about the remark I made about machines not talking nonsense," I said, "then I'm kind of sorry, but you did push me in a pool, so I thought we were even."

"I guess you're wrong there, Mac," replied Ari. She pushed the hatch open and swung herself out onto the ladder. Below us, I could see the shallow waters of the beach and the forested roof of the library.

"I'll see you later, Ari." She grunted and started her descent; and then I added hastily: "And I really am sorry about what I said!" But she was outside, and the wind and the engines drowned my voice. I watched her shape dwindle as she descended the ladder, and then she jumped off the bottom rung, landing on the roof of the palace. A moment later, she had vanished among the trees. I pulled in the ladder, closed the hatch, and returned to the wheel-house. Something in me regretted that I was heading to a different part of the island than Ari. But I shook all that sentimentality out of me and watched the land go by.

Soon, we passed over the golden wall and were flying over a wet area of interlocking lagoons, all fringed with trees. I saw palms and cypresses—the type that grow in swamps, not the tall and shapely ones you see in Italy and Greece. We came at last to a wide black wall against which the sea frothed and foamed. Sikorsky turned the wheel starboard, and we started following it north.

I leaned forward, peering through the fore-windows. Directly ahead, I could see what appeared to be a great thick tower rising from the wall. As we approached it, it resolved into a tall dome, at the summit of which was what looked like a gazebo. On the landward side, palms crowded against the base of the building.

I pointed. "There," I said, and Sikorsky brought the LS3 in low towards what appeared to be a wide and overgrown courtyard attached to the domed building. At the top of the wall, glazed windows ran around the whole circumference. Beneath them, appearing to grow out of the palms and spanning the space up to the bottoms of the windows, were a series of tall columns. It looked like a big bevel-gear.

"You are certain, McCracken?" asked Sikorsky. "Is here you wish to go?"

"I'm certain," I said. "Put me down in the court-yard."

Sikorsky pulled back on the throttle, eased the flaps up, and the airship came almost to a halt. I walked out into the passageway behind the wheel house. The Baron stood there, Fritz behind him.

"Good luck, Herr McCracken," said the Baron. "With you our hopes go. Find some orichalcum, *ja*?"

"I'll do my best," I replied.

"God go with you, Herr McCracken," added Fritz.

"Thank you, Fritz," I smiled. I double-checked my radio and adjusted the straps on my backpack, then slid out of the doorway and began to climb down the rope ladder. Above me, I heard the Baron's voice: "Herr Sikorsky, set a course north." Then I was on the ground.

I tapped the transmit button on the radio. "All right, Sikorsky," I said. "I'm safe. I'll speak to you at—" I flipped my wrist and consulted my watch, "—about nine-thirty."

"Is good, McCracken," came the Russian's voice. "Be safe and have good time, *da*?"

"*Da*," I said. The airship rose above me and set off into the north.

Around me grew thick trees and undergrowth, but through it all I could see the pillars on the side of the temple, and I made for them at once. Beneath my feet, I saw, flagstones had been laid by long-dead engineers, though now they were cracked and pushed up unevenly by the roots of trees, and grass sprouted from the cracks. I seemed to be walking along what had once been a wide avenue, with lines of statues on either side, each a couple of fathoms in height. Some wore crowns and wielded sceptres, others bore long and cruel-looking knives; some were robed, others bare-armed. Many of them were overgrown with vines, and age had crumbled their faces and fingers, so that they were the mere suggestion of men; others had been well preserved, so that you could read the pride impressed upon their features.

Before the doors of the temple, slightly ajar, was a wide terrace, and I climbed up to this now, my morning shadow stretching ahead of me. There were no trees up here, except the palms I had seen from above, which sprouted from the sandy ground immediately below the temple walls. I crept across the terrace and peered round the door.

The inside was softly lit, and it took my eyes a few moments to adjust. It was a wide circular room, tall as well. It was like being inside an empty soup can. About halfway between the floor and the apex of the domed roof, a balcony ran around the inner circumference, and the windows behind this balcony provided the soft light that gently illuminated the whole interior.

Opposite the door was a huge statue, once painted vividly, but the colours now cracked and fading. It depicted a man with a bull's head, that head lowered as if in contemplation. Not very nice contemplation. It was the image out of every child's reading: a minotaur.

Before the minotaur, at the centre of the circular floor, was a small round table, its top scored with soot—probably once an altar, upon which sacrificial offerings had been burned to the ghastly god that frowned down upon it. Without thinking about it, I made the Sign of the Cross.

As I looked in, the floor seemed to lurch, and I heard a muffled grinding and crunching noise. The temple shook for a few moments, and then was still again.

I wondered for a moment what could have produced the tremor, but my thoughts faded as the sun rose high enough to shine through the windows above the door. The light shone through the temple and struck the face of the statue. The minotaur's eyes flashed crimson, and a pair of beams lanced out from them, converging on the altar. A flame leaped from the table's surface about a foot and a half in the air, dancing and shimmering. I gasped, and took an involuntary step into the temple, for I knew I had discovered a pair of orichalcum fire stones.

CHAPTER 9
FETCHING THE FIRE STONES

I stood for a moment, lost in amazement, as the golden light of the sun was converted into twin beams of scarlet. The scarlet beams bored into the altar. I looked up, and saw that each of the windows on the balcony above had curtains or blinds of some sort, but that they had partially disintegrated and fallen away directly over my head. What I was seeing had not happened in four thousand years, since the last time the ancient priest had drawn back those blinds to let in the beams of the sun they worshipped, and—and what then? I looked at the altar. What sacrifices had it borne? Rams? Goats? Or something more gruesome?

I shuddered at the thought, but closed in on the altar anyway. The floor under my feet was a mosaic, but I couldn't see what it depicted. My eyes were riveted on the beams of concentrated light—concentrated enough to scorch the marble surface of the altar, to sear right through flesh.

I was now at the edge of the altar. The beams of light sang softly, with a sizzling sound, and I could smell ozone in the air. Suddenly, I remembered a young Swiss I had met a few years ago—Albert was his name, but at this moment, I couldn't recall his surname—who had been interested in the concept of the emission of electromagnetic radiation. He had thought that it would be possible to concentrate beams of light to an incredible intensity. I hadn't been able to follow most of his reasoning, in spite of my fine education at Imperial College, but I could recognize the fact that I was looking at his theory, now, made real. I resolved to write to him as soon as I was back in civilization.

But at that moment, the last fragment of the sun disappeared above the upper edge of the window, and the scarlet beams of light winked out, leaving a momentary whisper on the air. My eyes traveled through the air, through which the beams had passed just moments before, and up to the eyes of the statue. They were dull again.

I scanned the inside of the temple once more. The balcony, I saw, ran around the domed ceiling at roughly the level of the statue's shoulders. I should be able to climb onto it and take the fire stones. And there were doors in the walls at ground level, roughly at north and south. These perhaps concealed stair-wells leading to the balcony. I resolved to try one of them.

A few moments later, I emerged onto the balcony. The windows where the blinds had disintegrated afforded a wide prospect of the land below. To the east lay the undulating forest, to the west the shimmering blue of the Mediterranean. Directly ahead of me was the statue, grim and sinister. Quickly, I took off my backpack, found my rope and pulleys, and rigged a harness. I threaded it through my belt, then attached it to a lasso at one end and to the balcony railing at the other. I could extend or contract the line by pulling on or releasing the loose end of the rope as I wished. I swung the lasso over my head, and then flung it at the minotaur. It shivered over the horns, and I pulled on it until it was secure. Then I climbed up onto the balcony railing, and from there onto the statue's shoulder.

From up here, I could see the entirety of the mosaic clearly. It showed the sun and, silhouetted against it, a man with wings—Daedalus, no doubt, I thought.

The bull's head of the statue had a shock of rough and curly hair falling over its shoulders, and its locks were difficult for my boots to get a grip on. My feet slipped as I moved towards the head, and I wished I had taken my boots and socks off before undertaking this climb. Inch by inch, I edged across the shoulder towards the head. I could see the nearer of the orichalcum eyes, glaring down at the sun-sacrifice altar. Holding onto the rope with one hand, I reached out with the other. It wasn't quite within my grasp.

At that moment, the Temple of the Minotaur shook again. Once again came a sound like grinding gears, and a tremor ran through the temple walls and ceiling, and through the statue.

My foot slipped, and the rope seared through my fingers. I plunged through the air towards the floor. But the pulleys did their job, and I didn't reach terminal velocity. Rather, my feet gently touched the floor. I stood there for a moment, annoyed at the setback and not a little curious about these strange tremors. Then I slipped the rope out of my belt and headed back for the stairwell.

Once back on the balcony, I pulled up the rope and secured it again to my belt, then ventured cautiously out onto the beast's shoulder. Somewhere in the back of my mind, I was working on the problem of why the temple had shuddered like that, twice in less than an hour.

But the immediate problem allowed me no further speculation. I lifted my left foot, edged it twelve inches to the side, edged the right closer. With a mental imprecation, I realized that I had once again forgotten to remove my boots.

At last, I could place my feet on either side of the beast's chin. By releasing the rope slowly, I was able to climb down its chest until my face was level with its face. I slipped my arm around it, as if I were embracing it.

"Don't get any ideas, Mr. Minotaur," I said. "We're not engaged or anything."

Reaching out with my free hand, I tested the first eye. To my surprise, it came out easily. I tucked it into my pocket, and then pulled the other out. After all that, the fire stones were remarkably easy to remove. I swung a foot up onto the statue's shoulder once more, clambered up, and then slid back over to the balcony. My feet dropped to the floor on the other side of the railing, and I felt as if I could breathe again. In a few moments, I had disassembled the pulleys and rope, and they were safely stored in my backpack once more.

I took out the fire stones. They were identical in all ways to the one I had left behind in the airship—the same shape, the same size, the same weight. I transferred them into my pouch, and looked around. Time to explore the rest of the balcony, I thought, walking off behind the statue.

There was a small door behind the statue. I don't know why I thought it was so important—perhaps *because* it was so small, so hidden. I pushed gently on it, and found that it opened quite easily. Beyond it was a flight of stone steps, smooth and sharply-cut, as if they had rarely been used. I took the electric torch out of my backpack then, thumbing its switch, pointed the yellow beam down the steps and began my descent.

At first, the walls were as smoothly-cut as the steps. But after about thirty feet or so, the torch-beam showed rough-hewn walls of stone that dripped with seawater, like dark sweating flesh. The air was cold and clammy. And the stairwell began to turn to the right in a tight spiral.

Down I went, and down, and still more down. It seemed as if I would never come to the end of this twisting downward spiral. And the air was getting colder and damper. There was a musty smell to it. I wondered if I were the first human being to breathe this air in four thousand years.

Then, all at once, I came to a flat area. I shone the torch in either direction, and found I was in a chamber, about fifteen feet square. On the further side of it was a door.

I shone my light over the door. There didn't seem to be a handle or knob at all, and when I tested it, it proved to be firmly shut and locked. But in the middle of the door was a large circular panel of bronze, with a number of indentations in it of a familiar shape and size.

Excitement mounting in me, I drew out the fire stones, and inserted the first of them into one of the indentations. The bronze panel rotated, with a grinding noise, through 120 degrees. I slotted the next fire stone in, and the panel moved again. But there was a third slot, empty and mocking me. I tested the door; it was as firmly locked as it had been before. I cursed myself for not having brought my father's fire stone with me that day.

I turned to leave, and noticed for the first time that the ground was wet underfoot. More than wet, there must have been an inch of seawater over the floor. And as I moved towards the steps, placing the fire stones back into my pouch, I heard a grinding sound, just like I'd heard before, but immeasurably louder down here. At the same time, the chamber shook as if an earthquake were hitting it, and I heard a spurt of water from nearby as a crack in the wall admitted water from outside.

With rising horror, I realized at once that I was below sea-level, and that Thera was sinking again.

With all the speed I could muster, I dashed out and up the spiral steps, the pitching and swinging light from the torch ahead of me as I flew. At last, I came out onto the balcony and dashed to one of the windows. I pulled the blinds from it and looked out at the courtyard below.

All seemed peaceful and serene—there were as yet no visible signs that the island was sinking.

I descended to the main floor of the temple, and left through the main doors. Looking at the forested courtyard from the ground level, there were still no signs that Thera was sinking. My watch told me that the time was now ten-thirty—Sikorsky was an hour overdue. That was all right—one couldn't make precise plans under such circumstances. But I decided to climb up to the gazebo on the roof of the temple, if I could, to await him there, as the altitude would make the radio signal stronger, and he would not have to bring the LS3 in so low. So I started searching the balcony for steps going up. I soon found them, and emerged into a small circular space at the top of the temple's domed roof. It was open to the air, and a delightful breeze blew through it. I could see the sparkling ocean on one side, and the forest on the other as far as what looked like a wall of bronze. Visible over the top of that wall were the upper branches of more trees. Not for the first time, I wondered how Thera was irrigated with fresh water—we had seen the fresh water springs that emerged from the base of the Folly, but I was at a loss to explain how they got there. And I remembered what Jaubert had pointed out, that forests of such an extent would be an impossibility with nothing but salt water.

I flipped the transmit switch on my radio, and said, "Hello, Sikorsky. Come in, LS3, come in LS3."

The reply was static—nothing but static. I tried a few more times, then set it down against the inner wall of the gazebo. I took out my rosary and prayed the Sorrowful Mysteries (it was Friday) and, when I had finished, took out a book I had borrowed from the airship's library—it was just a little light reading, Henry T. Brown's *Mechanical Movements*—and began to read.

Everyone who knows Brown's book knows just what delightful reading it is, what infinite variety of diagrams and descriptions the enchanted reader finds within its relatively few pages, and when I finally looked at my watch, I found to my surprise that nearly an hour had passed. The LS3 still had not shown up. I took out the lunch Fritz had packed for me, and ate it slowly. Fritz had called it *Krabbenbrötchen*: fresh lettuce leaves, mounds of crab, and a tangy sauce in which I could taste garlic, dill, and cayenne pepper. I ate slowly to savour Fritz's cuisine, still browsing Henry's charming pages, but occasionally now getting up and scanning the horizon for the airship. The breeze stiffened a little, bringing in clouds from the west, and the sun climbed to its zenith.

Another hour passed, and I was beginning to get concerned. I had re-packed my book, and tried the radio again, but still there was nothing but static. I leaned over the parapet and examined the courtyard below. I sketched its plan, which was clearer from up here than from below. The walls were not straight—they fanned out on either side, and the outer wall was a wide arc with the gates in the centre. There had been shady colonnades along either side, and the terracotta roofs were broken in places, so that I could see the pavements through the holes.

I spent another hour mapping the courtyard, then descended the steps to the temple. I paced the whole circumference, and sketched the entire thing, its plan and side-elevations. That took longer than I expected, and it was almost four o'clock in the afternoon when I was finished. And it was then that the static on the radio finally resolved into Sikorsky's voice.

"McCracken, McCracken, are you there? Come in, McCracken."

I thumbed down the transmit switch. "McCracken here, Sikorsky. Good to hear your voice."

"Is good to hear you too, McCracken. Sorry for delay—Miss Bell is in trouble."

"What kind of trouble?" I demanded in rising fear.

"Not bad," answered Sikorsky quickly. "She need water turbine at library. We are many hours removing water from it."

"It doesn't surprise me," I replied. "It looks as if the whole island is sinking."

"Is stranger than that," answered Sikorsky, "but I tell you when I see you—I arrive at temple in four minutes."

"I'll be in the gazebo," I said. "McCracken out."

By the time I emerged onto the gazebo once more, the LS3 was already close. Her flaps were down, and she was nosing towards me. The Baron stood in the doorway, and he kicked the rope ladder out. I reached out, took it, and climbed into the gondola. I nodded a greeting to the Baron and strode into the wheel-house, where Sikorsky was easing the LS3 away from the gazebo.

"McCracken," he said, "is very good seeing you."

"You too," I replied. "Is everybody on board?"

Sikorsky let out on the throttle and the hum of the engines rose. "Miss Bell is in cabin—she has Theran . . . I do not know word in English. *Napisanie tabletki.*"

"Tablet?"

"*Da*, she have tablets, many of them, with writing all over. She is in cabin, translating."

"That'll make her happy," I commented, with perhaps a hint of irony. "Hours of fun. How about Jaubert?"

"Jaubert is still in marshes—we go there now to pick him up, and then back to Folly."

"Good," I said. "Now, what's stranger than Thera sinking again?"

Below us, the cigar-shaped shadow of the airship flitted over the tree-tops. Sikorsky said, "You map Thera, McCracken. You know where things are." I nodded. "This temple you are in today, is due west, *da*?"

"That's what I reckoned," I agreed.

"Well, is not any more. Now, temple is ten points north of due west."

"Ah!" I said. The Baron, I saw, had joined us.

"You have a solution to the mystery, Herr McCracken?" he asked.

"Well, it seems easy enough to deduce," I told them. "Thera was raised on some kind of gigantic screw-thread, which explains its revolving as it came up out of the sea; now it's sinking again, and un-screwing." I told them about the chamber in the Temple of the Minotaur that was rapidly becoming water-logged. "My guess is that we'll be needing the water turbines a lot, after all."

"How fast does Thera sink, McCracken?" asked Sikorsky.

"Hard to say without more information," I answered.

"But why does this happen, Herr McCracken?" asked the Baron.

I spread my hands. "It's old machinery, Baron," I explained, "very old. I'd guess the four-thousand-year-old cogs and wheels and gears are getting a wee bit worn out."

"You can repair it, though?" inquired the Baron.

"Well, I don't know without seeing it. We'd have to find it and, until then, use the water turbines to drain places locally, while we explore."

The Baron's eye glinted. "And what did you find today, Herr McCracken?" he asked.

I took the new fire stones out of my pouch and showed them to him. "They're keys that work in combination to unlock a door below the temple. Unfortunately, I needed three, and I left my own in my cabin," I explained.

Here Sikorsky chimed in again. "McCracken," he said, "we see much orichalcum today. This morning, the Baron and I, we go to Orichalcum Wall. Is made of big square plates, a foot on each side and two inches thick, and these the Therans bolt into stone wall. Where we are, many orichalcum plates are on ground, and a few other things as well. Is very mysterious—sometimes, this orichalcum look like metal, sometimes like gem."

"I imagine it's something to do with its thickness," I suggested. "How did they get it, I wonder? And how did they shape it? By chiseling, or by moulds? There are enough mysteries for a lifetime on this island! But tomorrow morning, I'm taking the three fire stones we've found to the temple, to see what's below it."

But at that moment, a roar of static burst from the radio speaker. We all flinched, and Sikorsky hit the transmit button. "Jaubert, Jaubert, is that you?"

"Sikorsky!" cried Jaubert. "Sikorsky—come quickly! There is—"

But his voice was cut short. He may have cried out in fear or pain, but the transmission was cut short. We all looked at each other with wild eyes. Sikorsky began trying to get hold of him again, but nothing came from the speakers.

We had totally lost Jaubert.

I pulled on the diving suit that hung from its peg in the workshop, then clattered down the steps to the passageway behind the wheel-house. Sikorsky called over his shoulder, "McCracken, you are there?"

"I'm here. How long?"

"One minute, perhaps two, to rendezvous point. Be ready."

I strapped the rebreather to my back, and fitted the helmet over my head. The Baron tightened the nuts around the rim of the helmet. As I watched through the helmet's portholes, I saw Ari joining us. She directed a question at the Baron, who replied, but their words were muffled by my helmet. The Baron turned back to me, unscrewed the helmet again and lifted it from my head.

"What's happening?" I asked, struggling to keep my irritation under control.

"Fraulein Bell," explained the Baron, "a plan she has devised."

Ari had taken the helmet, and was doing something inside it with a screwdriver. As she worked, she explained, "I'm setting your radio to the same frequency as Jaubert's. It won't give you a direction,

117

but the signal will get stronger as you close in on him. The only problem is that we won't be able to talk to you, nor you to us—for this to work, Jaubert's radio has to be the only one you're listening to." She handed the helmet back. "The sun will be setting in about an hour and a half," she added. "We don't have any lights that will work underwater, so that's the limit of your time down there. And that's the rebreather I was using today. It isn't fully recharged, but I wasn't using it much, so you should be okay. But I'm concerned about Jaubert. He may have less than an hour left in his rebreather." I nodded my understanding. Ari said, "God be with you," and I replaced the helmet over my head. Ari tightened the screws, then looked up through the for'ard porthole into my eyes. There was a quick smile of encouragement with her lips, and a look of concern in her eyes.

The Baron unlocked the door and pushed it open. The marshes lay below us, the lake golden in the lowering sun. A flight of herons was winging leisurely across it. I said a quick prayer and lowered myself out of the door and down the rope-ladder. Sikorsky had slowed the LS3 to near a crawl, and there was almost no slipstream as I climbed down.

At length, I was just a few feet above the water, and I released my grip. At once, I felt the impact with the water, and bubbles were streaming past the portholes. I looked down at my feet, gauged the distance to the lake-bed, and bent my knees for the impact. It came a little sooner than I expected, and I bounced, but landed on my feet.

The radio was silent, just a faint hiss. I said, "Jaubert, Jaubert, are you there? Come in." Randomly selecting a direction, I started walking, my steps slow and buoyant. I could see tangled weeds in all directions, an undulating landscape of dunes. Long silver shapes slid through the water—eels and other kinds of fish. The water was muddy, so I could barely see twenty yards.

"Come in, Jaubert," I said.

I felt a great eddy wash over me, and at the same time, a large shadow passed by overhead. There was no upper porthole in the helmet, so it took a moment to adjust my head so that I could look up at it. But when I had done that, there was nothing to see.

"Jaubert, are you there?" I said into the radio. Nothing. I tried gathering together the scraps of French I'd learned in school, and repeated myself as far as I could in Jaubert's language: "*Êtes-vous là, mon ami?*" Perhaps it was my imagination, but the static hiss seemed to be a little louder.

Something dark, like a large snake, appeared briefly in my left porthole. Startled, I turned to face whatever it was. But my movement was too sharp, and I went spiraling down to the lake-bed in a plume of sand. I won't tell you what I said—probably nobody would want to print it.

It took me a few moments to struggle to my feet. "Jaubert," I said, "are you there? What did you see, you crazy Frenchman? Was it a giant snake?"

I started walking again, though I wasn't sure if I was going in the right direction. For all I knew, I might be retracing the route by which I had got there—I had no sense of direction under the water. I talked the whole way, turning my head left and right to scan the waters for any large snakelike shapes. The minutes stretched, the light grew dimmer, and I saw nothing, heard nothing, except the static.

But I thought the static was louder now.

At that moment, I saw a dark shape ahead of me. It dived down from above my line of sight, and was heading directly for me. I had a fleeting impression of a turtle-like shape, with flat fins out on either side, and a bulky body, except that it was far larger than a turtle. All this takes a long time to describe, but I saw it for only a fraction of a second, and then it was gone overhead. I caught a glimpse of a long tail. I tried to turn, but I had learned my lesson from earlier, and did so slowly. It had already vanished into the gloomy waters.

"Jaubert," I said, "where are you? Come in, Jaubert, please!" A sound came over the radio. It sounded a little like a groan. "Jaubert? Jaubert! I think I can hear you. Come in, please. Where are you?"

Another groan, and then: "McCracken, *c'est toi*?"

"Yes, Jaubert, it's me!" I cried. "Where are you?"

"*Excusez-moi*, I cannot tell where is me," replied the Frenchman. "I am at the bottom of this lake, but I cannot tell what has happened."

"I must be close to you," I said. "Your signal is strong. Are you standing?"

"*Non*," replied Jaubert. "Something it has knocked me down. I think it must have been—how you say?—*évanoui*."

"Unconscious," I suggested. "We have to get back to the surface—the batteries in your rebreather won't last much longer."

A stream of irritable French came over the radio. "Yes," he said in English at last, "I know this—I invent the rebreather, I know how long it will last."

"Sorry, Jaubert," I said. "Of course you know how long it will last."

"I accept your apology, monsieur," replied Jaubert. "Please forgive my unpleasant words. I am standing now. You can see me?"

I slowly turned through 360 degrees, and again, and then— "Yes, I can see you!" I said. The figure was indistinct in the cloudy waters. "I think," I added.

Just then, some huge shadow sped past me, obscuring Jaubert from me for a moment. I glimpsed a long, slender neck, a bulbous body, and two sets of

121

flippers, flicking through the water. It was hard to estimate in the growing gloom, but it looked as if it were thirty or forty feet long.

"Great Scott!" I cried out.

"Ah, McCracken!" replied Jaubert. I could see him again now. "Then you have seen it?"

"I've seen something," I said. I was striding slowly towards him now—it was definitely Jaubert. "Do you know what it is?"

"*Mais oui*," replied Jaubert. "It is the thing which is striking me down and causing me to be unconscious. I think it intended no harm to me, though—it eats only *l'herb*—the plants."

"That's a huge creature," I said. "I've never seen anything like it before."

"No one has seen one for many millions of years," said Jaubert. "It is a plesiosaur. Ah, *pardon, monsieur, pardon!* You have possibly seen one of these creatures in your native country. Have you never been to—how you say?—Loch Ness?"

I had soon joined Jaubert, and together we watched as Nessie returned twice more. She was a graceful creature, lithe enough in her own element, a perfect underwater machine. She was also friendly, swimming close to us, and forcing us to duck to avoid getting smacked by one of her flippers. But we couldn't stay long, for all that I would have liked it. The light was growing dim, and Jaubert was getting short of air, so we returned to the surface, and found ourselves soon in the LS3.

We all assembled in the *Speiseraum* that evening, and Fritz, who seemed to be in a particularly Germanic mood, served us a delightful repast of soft and tender meatballs and potatoes in a creamy white sauce, which he called Königsberger Klopsch, spicy-sweet red cabbage and a sweet soup made from beetroot, with pumpernickel bread rolls on the side. We ate heartily, for we had had an active day. Outside the windows of the LS3, the lost island was shrouded in darkness, but we had left the windows open to cool the gondola down, and we could hear the nighttime sounds—the tree-frogs, the crickets, and the occasional call of some beastie awoken from its rest.

"And now, *meine Fraulein und Herren*," said the Baron, as we finished with Fritz's marzipan hearts, each studded with a cherry and dusted lightly with confectioner's sugar, "what have we discovered today?"

Ariadne reached below the table and brought out a briefcase. She placed this on the table, opened it out, and drew out a dozen clay tablets, all about the size of my hand. They were etched with scores of tiny symbols, too various to be a regular alphabet, and some of them looked like pictures rather than letters. One of them was a disc, the characters spiraling towards the centre. "Obviously, it's a hieroglyphic system for the most part," Ari told us. "That makes it occasionally easy: when I see a pictogram of a bird, it's a fair bet that symbol means *bird*. But some of them are taxograms—things you can't represent pictorially, like the names of gods and goddesses, mythological heroes, abstract ideas like love, hate, fear, envy. Those are difficult to decode, and I need to use the context to interpret them." She had passed the tablets round the table, and we examined them briefly and passed them on. "Others of these symbols are puns," she went on. "In English, we might draw a picture of an eye to represent the first-person pronoun *I*. Since I have only the vaguest knowledge of the Minoan language's vocabulary, that takes a lot of time."

"Have you been able to translate any of it?"

"Of course," replied Ari, "but not much yet." She paused, and looked at each one of us in turn. "I know we haven't spent long here," she said, "but has anyone seen any evidence of human remains here?" We all looked at one another questioningly. "At Pompeii," Ari went on, "excavators discovered hundreds of bodies. They discovered that there were cavities beneath the surface of the earth, and by filling them with plaster, were able to make perfect moulds of the inhabitants of Pompeii. They were all over the city, mostly trying to escape the eruption of the volcano. We know from the Younger Pliny that hundreds actually managed to escape. But we haven't discovered any bodies on Thera. Everyone seems to have gotten away—everyone."

She gave us a few seconds to absorb this observation.

"When Thera was destroyed by this volcano," said Ari, "the Therans knew of it well enough in advance that they could all leave, every last one of them. They knew it was coming."

"How?" I asked. "From what I understand, nobody in Pompeii saw the eruption coming. They were caught completely unawares."

"That's true," agreed Ari. "My theory is that the Therans knew the blast was coming because they caused it." Nobody asked anything. We couldn't guess where Ari was going. "The Therans were a nation of engineers," explained Ari.

"I like them better already," I interjected.

"Whatever disadvantage that might have to one's personal life," Ari continued, "they were certainly good at what they did. They developed machinery that could raise and lower the island on a gigantic screw-thread. It's possible that it was putting that strain on the natural geology of the area that *caused* the eruption that destroyed the island."

"Or perhaps," I suggested, anxious to defend the ancient engineers, "after an eruption they didn't foresee, they built the screw-thread to keep the island tight down on the volcano, like a cork in a bottle, so that it wouldn't erupt again. And then they left."

"You're the engineer, Mac," said Ari mildly. "You would know if that's possible."

"Not with the technology we possess today," I admitted. "But with today's technology, we can't raise a whole island, fifty miles in diameter—and we saw that happen less than a week ago."

"What is this symbol, mademoiselle?" asked Jaubert, pointing to something on the clay tablet he held.

"That looks like a drinking horn," said Ari, "and that's probably what it means. It's odd, though—it seems to have wings or something."

"*Oui, vraiment*," agreed Jaubert. "It is most strange, which is why I recognized it, because this I saw today, mademoiselle, on the bottom of the lake."

"This very thing?" said Ari.

"*Oui, mademoiselle*," said Jaubert. "And then I am thinking, we all remember the book written by Monsieur Edgar Elde? The book about Atlantis? He spoke of the Horn of Tempests, which could be found in the Temple of Apollo?"

"I remember that, Jaubert," I said, "but I also remember that it was contained in a temple at the perimeter of Atlantis. And this was not at the perimeter, nor in a temple."

"Quite correct, monsieur," admitted Jaubert. "I cannot explain what I saw, only observe that I saw it.

126

It is there, I assure you; the problem is, how will we raise it? It is *très lourd*—very heavy."

"Perhaps Mac should go down with you tomorrow, Nicolas," suggested Ari. "I'll stay on the LS3, and see if I can make any more sense of these tablets."

So, the next morning, instead of returning to the Temple of the Minotaur, I dived into the lake with Jaubert. It took us an hour to find the fallen artifact Jaubert had described, but in the end there it was, just as he had described it: a horn, such as you would use to drink wine in ancient times, but huge and with wings growing from it halfway between tip and lip.

"I shall keep watch for Madame Nessie, *n'est-ce pas*?" said Jaubert.

"All right, Jaubert," I said. "I'll take a look at it."

I stooped over it. It had been chiseled out of marble, and was about six feet long. I tested the weight, and found I couldn't budge it an inch. It was built on a pedestal, most of which had broken off, presumably as it fell. I looked around. There, off to my right, were fallen fragments of what looked like a column—smooth, unlike the grooved Doric column, and tapering towards the base; we had started calling them Minoan Columns. I walked towards the fallen column and, a few feet from the statue, found a slab of marble, about ten feet square, protruding from the sand. When I looked closely at it, I saw that there was writing along the edge, exactly like the writing on Ari's clay tablets.

"It's too bad Ari isn't here," I lamented.

"*Pardonnez-moi?*" asked Jaubert.

"Oh, nothing, nothing at all," I said. "Come and see this."

Jaubert bounded over to join me, and we looked at the inscription together. After a few moments, Jaubert tried to move the slab. I held the other side and heaved, but all we managed to do was get it out of the sand. The inscription, we saw, was the same on each of the four sides, as if a short but urgent message were being communicated to all four points of the compass.

"I wish I could memorize all this gibberish," I said, pointing to the inscription.

"What is your opinion, Monsieur McCracken?" asked Jaubert. "Can we lift it, or the statue?"

"It would take a while," I said, "and our time might be better spent elsewhere. But Ari will want to see this inscription."

Once we were out of the water, the LS3 was easily within range of our radios, and within minutes she appeared. The rope ladder snaked out from the door, and Ari clambered down as quickly as she was able. I handed her my diving suit, and she pulled it quickly on.

"Have you made much progress with the language this morning?" I asked.

"Some," she replied. "It's very similar to Egyptian hiero—"

"I see," I said, fitting the helmet over her head and tightening the screws. "Tell me all about it when you get back up."

Ari and Jaubert waded into the lake, and I watched as the water slowly climbed up their sides and they were submerged. They could speak to one another, but not to me—for that I would have to return to the airship. It was my intention to maintain communication with Ari and Jaubert from the radio in the wheel-house. But to my surprise, I found that the rope ladder was no longer there. Perplexed, I looked up at the airship. As I watched, the LS3 turned its nose and headed off into the south, leaving me alone on the shore of the lake, and Ari and Jaubert's communications completely severed.

CHAPTER 11
A TREK THROUGH THE MARSHES

My first impulse was to chase after the airship on foot, but almost immediately I realized that that was futile—the normal cruising speed of the LS3 was about fifty miles an hour. I couldn't believe Sikorsky would do that to us, though it took relatively little effort to imagine the Baron giving such orders. What could his motives have been?

Then I remembered that I had left the fire stones behind, in my cabin. Had he gone off to the Temple of the Minotaur to explore by himself? It seemed unlike the Baron—he had never struck me as one willing to take many risks.

I returned to the shore of the lake. The land about here was bleak—nothing but wiry, knee-length grass, and stretches of brown muck. The margin of the lake itself was all mud, the mockery of a beach, wide and shining like a besmeared mirror. I saw little brown birds with curved beaks rooting around among the reeds and along the shore. I could hear frogs croaking, and from time to time saw snakes slithering through the slime. I noticed all this because I had nothing else to do, having left my backpack in the LS3. I paced back and forth on the shore of the lake, fuming, sometimes silently, but not always. And I waited for over two hours.

When two hours had passed, the surface of the lake stirred and two figures emerged, dripping, and waded through the water, then the mud, to the shore. I unscrewed Ari's helmet first, and she looked up at the sky.

"Where's the LS3?" she asked.

"Ah!" I said. "There's a question." I loosened the screws of Jaubert's helmet. "I don't know," I added. "They just flew away as soon as you went under."

"Flew away? Why?"

"I don't know. It wasn't part of the plan."

"And now?" wondered Jaubert. "What is it we do now?"

"We could try to make our way back to the Folly," suggested Ari. "It's only about half a mile." We concurred, but folded up the diving suits and stacked them on the ground with the helmets and rebreathers—we would go faster without the encumbrance, and could always come back for them later.

It was indeed only half a mile to the base of the Folly, as the airship flies; but in fact, scores of little waterways intersected our course, and trekking round them must have tripled the distance we hiked. Not only that, but the sun was getting high now, so that the air became hot as well as moist, and we began to sweat profusely as we laboured along ground that looked flat, but was in fact lumpy and soft, so that our boots often got stuck in mud.

We reached the base of Russian's Folly almost two hours after we had set out from the lake, to find that the steps began somewhere else, and that we would have to walk around to them. The news did not improve our tempers, but we said nothing and began wordlessly to hike clockwise around the base of the Folly.

"So," I said, "what did you find out about the Horn of Tempests?"

"Watch out!" said Ari. I stopped instantly and looked down at my feet: an inch away from another quicksand pit.

I shrugged. "I'm told it's pretty easy to get out of quicksand," I observed, as we walked on, taking a route around the pit.

After we had walked a few moments in silence, Ari began to explain, "The marble statue on the lake-bed isn't the original. The inscription was written by one Kitanetos, a priest of the Temple of Ariadne."

"Temple of what?"

"Of Ariadne." She threw a smug grin over her shoulder at me.

"So you're a goddess now?"

"Well, you remember how in Greek mythology Ariadne helps Theseus get through the labyrinth to the minotaur. It seems she was named after the goddess."

"I suppose there's no Minoan god called McCracken?" I wondered. "He would be the god of dashing good looks, devastating intelligence and engineering genius."

"Well, the Greeks had a kraken, anyway," said Ari mildly.

"What was he the god of?" I asked.

"Nothing. It was a giant squid, a monster." We walked on in silence for a while, and then Ari asked, "But perhaps you have another name?"

I slapped my neck. "The mosquitoes are terrible here," I said. We were threading our way through treacherous pools, and the ground repeatedly gave way beneath our feet. "So the original Horn of Tempests is in this temple?" I asked.

"*Oui*," said Jaubert. "Tomorrow I go there and find the Horn."

"So where is this Temple of . . . I forget the name," I said. "Where is it? Stop!" I called out. We had reached a dead-end: a small lake lay before us, a faint yellow mist rising from its glassy surface. "Left or right?" I wondered.

Ari pointed right, and we resumed our trek. "My guess would be that the Temple of Ariadne is at the perimeter of Thera," said Ari, "opposite the Temple of the Minotaur."

I nodded. "I think I've seen it from the air. It's built on a spur of rock, looks a bit like a pagoda."

"*Oui, naturellement,*" agreed Jaubert. "I too have seen this temple from the air."

We had been walking through the marshes for over three hours at this point, and at last saw trees ahead of us. I could even see the steps as they wound up the pillar of the Folly. They seemed to be taunting us.

We plodded on through the marshes and, shortly after that, plunged into the forest. The sun was high overhead, and it shone directly on the green canopy over our heads, turning what was below into a veritable greenhouse. If anything, it was worse than the marshes, though there weren't mosquitoes here. The sounds of the animals were deafening in all directions.

"I can't believe those . . . those . . . *folks* left us stranded," Ari commented bitterly. "I can't believe Vasili would do that to us."

"I do not believe Sikorsky abandoned us willingly," Jaubert said. "The Baron—I do not trust him. It is never I can see his eyes."

"The Germans and the French have never got along well," I said.

"It is not that, monsieur," replied Jaubert in a dignified way that made me ashamed to have spoken like that. "I have met many *Allemands*, some I like, some I do not like. This one I do not trust."

"I think there's going to be a bit of a disagreement soon," I observed.

"But no, monsieur," said Jaubert. "I will start no fisticuffs, nor I think you, nor mademoiselle here."

"That's not what I mean," I said. "I think all over Europe, there will be big disagreements soon—it'll be us, and you French, and the Russians, and perhaps the Americans too, against the Germans. It's been building up for a while."

No one said anything for a long while after this. The birds twittered in the trees, the dragonflies buzzed to and fro across our path, and a parrot like a glowing emerald arced through the air overhead. Then, so quietly we could almost not hear him, Jaubert said, "I very much fear it to be true, Monsieur McCracken. It is as if the lights they are going off, all over Europe."

At that moment, the jungle trembled slightly, as if it were being shaken by a mild earthquake. The tremor startled a cloud of squawking birds out of the upper branches of some of the trees, and a few leaves drifted down from the canopy to the forest floor. We exchanged glances.

"That was like those tremors I felt yesterday in the Temple of the Minotaur," I said. "Not quite so strong."

"Thera," said Jaubert, "she is sinking, I think, *n'est-ce pas?*"

"If we don't find what the Baron wants soon," I said, "I think we'll be getting very wet."

"How long do you think we have, Mac?" asked Ari.

"I can't be certain," I replied. "Yesterday, Sikorsky told me that the island had rotated through ten degrees since it first rose. That would be a rate of between two and three degrees per day. But I doubt if the rate will be constant. It will speed up as the old machinery loses its grip."

On we went. And, shortly after, the trees started to thin out, and we came to a wide gorge, at the bottom of which flowed a river. A fine mist hung over the whole scene, for the river emerged from the cliff-face of the Folly not at the base, but a couple of hundred feet up, and the spray fountained high up into the air. The walls of the gorge were mostly bare rock, rising in jagged pillars all about and glistening with the water. A descent right there would be dangerous and time-consuming.

"There's a bridge further down there," I said, shouting above the roar of the falls and pointing off to the left.

The sound of the falls muted slightly as we all trooped south, following the course of the river. The ground was uneven, and we had to go slowly and carefully. I kept my eye on the sky, hoping all the time to see the LS3 sailing towards us, and wondering what on earth could have motivated Sikorsky to abandon us like that.

136

Presently, we reached a waist in the gorge, narrow enough to be spanned by a rope bridge. When I looked at it closer, I saw it was constructed from cable rather than rope, spun from fine threads of what looked like copper. It and the planking were green with the incessant spray. The cables were held in place by a pair of stout poles at either end. The further side was considerably higher than the near one, so to cross the bridge would be to climb a slight gradient as we did so.

Ari peered over the edge of the gorge at the foaming river below. "It's going to break halfway across," she said. "That's how it always goes in the stories."

"Yesterday," I said, "you were making fun of me for reading too many adventure stories about quicksand. Now who's been reading too many adventure stories?"

"Enough of this foolishness," said Jaubert, and started off across the bridge. It bounced and swayed as he moved. I flashed Ari a smile and started out myself. After a slight paused, she followed.

Walking across the bridge was kind of like walking across a fisherman's net, and I have to admit that it was somewhat unnerving to be so far from the river below and standing on what felt so much like an unstable platform. But I had faith in those ancient engineers.

Nevertheless, I prayed about a dozen Hail Marys as we crossed.

About a third of the way across, the whole place shuddered again. The bridge swayed from side to side as well as up and down. Ari cried out and wrapped the cable of the bridge around her forearm until the tremor had died away. I looked back at her over my shoulder. "Are you all right back there?"

She was as white as wool. "Just carry on," she said. "I'll be right behind you."

We moved off again, a little more rapidly than before, and the bridge bounced under our feet. When I looked ahead, I could see waves caused by our footsteps moving through the slats and cables.

Jaubert reached the further side. I stepped onto firm land. And then it happened.

Another minor earthquake shook the whole landscape. It cast me and Jaubert to the ground. Ahead of us, in the forest, surprised birds rose in cacophonous clouds from the trees. A column of rock not far from us shivered into pieces that went whirling down the gorge into the river below. One of the cables of the bridge was wrenched from the pole supporting it, and the bridge did a flip. Ari screamed.

"Ari!" I yelled.

But she had disappeared.

CHAPTER 12
A DESCENT INTO THE CAVES

I dived for the edge of the cliff. Fragments of rock were still tumbling towards the seething river beneath. The bridge was still in place, but the breaking of the rope had flipped it about so that nobody would ever cross on it again. And Ari was not there. She was gone.

I felt as if a part of me had fallen down the cliff, and I lay there, my hands extended over the edge, unmoving. I couldn't believe she was gone. Slowly, my movements agonized, I hauled myself into a sitting position.

"Monsieur McCracken?" Jaubert had joined me at the edge and spoke in a voice I could barely hear over the turbulent sound of the falls. I had my face in my hands. "Monsieur McCracken, I am so sorry."

"There were all sorts of things I wanted to say to her," I said.

"Like what?"

It wasn't Jaubert's voice. I leaped up and peered over the edge. Ari was clinging to the side of the cliff, partly hidden by the rock to which she was clinging, which is why I hadn't seen her before.

"Ari! Thank heaven!" I cried. Then I said more calmly, "Whatever are you doing there?"

"Waiting for a real man to help me up," answered Ari, grunting slightly with the effort of holding on. "I may as well just jump."

"Would you like a rope?" I asked.

"If you could spare one," she replied.

I took some out of my backpack and lowered the end over the edge. She took hold of it and, with me and Jaubert taking the strain, climbed up to join us.

I coiled the rope up and returned it to my backpack. "Well," I said, dusting my hands off, "shall we be going?"

The forest began again twenty yards or so from the head of the bridge. We entered, the green shadows closing about us and the birdsong enveloping us in its embrace.

"So," said Ari, "what were those things you wanted to say to me?"

"Oh, just some thoughts I had about improving the radios, that's all." I crooked my elbow for her.

"I see." She slipped her arm through mine. "Mac," she said, "what's your first name?"

We walked on for a few paces without saying anything, then I pointed through the trees. "Look," I said, "there are the steps we're looking for."

They were quite close now. We glimpsed them more and more frequently through the trees, until we finally made it to the foot of the Folly and began climbing. It was quite a relief to climb above the tops of the trees, where it was just hot, and not also wet and humid.

The higher we got, the more Thera opened up below us. We could see the forest below us, like a field of broccoli, to the south.

The resemblance of the forest to broccoli reminded me of how hungry I was, and I growled along with my stomach. Whatever emergency Sikorsky and the Baron had faced had taken Fritz's cooking away from us.

We ascended the pillar of rock further, and the marshes came into view, concealed by its thin layer of mist. By the time we had made a complete circuit of the Folly, we were nearly halfway up it, and Jaubert pointed, shouting with some excitement, "Mademoiselle Bell, Monsieur McCracken, *regardez!*"

Out of the west was coming the thin pencil-shape of the airship. We kept on climbing, our muscles screaming at us for the effort. For a while, the LS3 was lost to sight while we were on the far side of the rocky column, but at length we stepped out onto the plateau of the Folly, where we were surrounded by the ruined walls and columns of the Theran palace, and there was the LS3 ahead of us. She had already descended almost to a landing, but no lines were deployed to secure her. The door to the gondola was open, and Sikorsky was beckoning us wildly. We hastened along the dusty streets, but having just ascended six or seven hundred feet's worth of steps, we could hardly run; at last, we climbed up into the gondola.

"What happened?" I asked.

"McCracken," said Sikorsky, "is very bad, and I am sorry I am leaving you this morning. The Baron, he has his orders."

"From whom?"

"From himself, for me."

"Where did you go?" asked Ari.

"Temple of Minotaur. Come with me into wheel-house." He led us for'ard—I stopped by the galley to grab some salami and cheese, which I stuffed into my backpack for later—and when we were all gathered, he eased up the throttle and took the LS3 up and away from the Folly. His touch on the controls was deft and gentle and the massive airship responded willingly.

"Is very bad situation," Sikorsky said. "The Baron, he tell me, 'Go to Temple of Minotaur,' so I go, and drop him and Fritz off there. He have orichalcum stones. He and Fritz, they enter Temple, but they do not come out again."

"Did you look for them?"

"*Da*," said the Russian. "I secure LS3 with anchor, I go into Temple of Minotaur, down steps, into chamber, under much water. I find door, with orichalcum stones in it. But Baron and Fritz, they are not there, and they are not in chamber beyond. I cannot tell where they are gone."

"Okay," I said, "take me and Ari to the Temple of the Minotaur, and then take Jaubert to the lake to get the rebreathers back. Then take him to the Temple of Ariadne." Sikorsky raised an eyebrow. "Yes, the Minoans worshipped a goddess called Ariadne. It's hard for me to believe as well."

"It sounds perfectly reasonable to me," said Ari. "The Horn of Tempests is at the Temple of Ariadne." Sikorsky nodded his understanding.

"Ari," I said, "come with me. I think we'll need one of the water turbines."

We ran up the steps into the workshop, where my four water turbines lay side by side in a corner. One of us could have carried it alone, with some effort, but there was no need. We each picked up an end and carried it back towards the steps.

"Mac," said Ari, as we laboured down the steps with the turbine, "what were you going to say about improving the radios?"

"Oh, I don't remember," I answered. "I reckon it wasn't important."

We set the turbine down carefully beside the outer door. As I straightened up, I found she had grabbed me by the collar of my shirt. Reaching up, she kissed me swiftly, but not on the nose this time.

"What was that for?" I asked in surprise.

"Oh, I don't know," she replied, mimicking my accent, "I reckon it wasn't important."

"Not important!" I fumed. "What if I wanted to kiss you back?"

"Ladies don't kiss gentlemen whose first names they don't know," she said primly.

I was in the midst of formulating a witty reply when Jaubert hurried out of the wheel-house. "Monsieur, mademoiselle," he said, "we have arrived at the Temple of the Minotaur."

And the LS3 began its descent towards the dome, silhouetted against the setting sun.

It took us a while to get the equipment out of the airship, and the shadows had lengthened and engulfed the world before we finished setting up the water turbines in the underground chamber. The hose snaked up the steps, across the floor of the temple, out of the door and over the wall, so that the waters gushed back into the Mediterranean. When the pumping was underway, Ari said, "So, why didn't they take the fire stones out of the door?"

"My guess is that if you take any of the stones out of the lock, it closes. So you have to leave the key in the door." I waded across to the door—the water was now down to waist-height—and pried one of the stones out of the door. It instantly swung closed, and wouldn't budge. "Clever, really. It makes sure you never lock yourself out." I took the torch out of my backpack and thumbed the switch. "Well, there's no sense in delaying. Are you coming?"

In reply, Ari took out her torch and switched it on. I replaced the stone, and together, we pulled open the door and ventured inside.

As Vasili had said, there was indeed a chamber beyond, its floor awash now that we had opened the outer door. I shone my light over the walls and ceiling. There were no features—it seemed to be nothing more than an empty space with blank walls.

"This can't be right," I reasoned, stepping close to the far wall. A closer examination revealed that there were actually patterns in it, but they were hard to see because they were shallow indentations rather than a painted design. It was a series of squares going from top to bottom in what looked like a random way. "What could that mean?" I wondered.

Ari ran her fingers along one of the square indentations. "Perhaps if we press them in a certain order, a door will open."

"I see. Sort of like an ancient combination lock?" For a little while, we tried pressing the indentations in one order or another, but there were a lot of them, and millions of possible combinations. In any case, the indentations themselves seemed to have no moving parts.

"Maybe this isn't the mechanism," suggested Ari. "Maybe this is just a clue."

As she said it, I glanced down at the floor. It was dry now, and I could see that it was made up of square tiles. "That's it!" I declared. "It *is* a clue, not the lock itself!"

I strode back to the door, and stepped on the floor tile immediately before it. When I pressed with my foot, it sank slightly. Then, looking up at the pattern on the wall, I stepped diagonally to another tile, which also gave a little under my weight, and then to another, and then another. Sometimes, the patterns on the wall guided me to step backwards, sometimes sideways, sometimes straight, sometimes diagonally. But the pattern on the wall was my guide, and it brought me in the end to the other side of the chamber. At which point—

With a grinding noise, the whole wall moved upwards and into the ceiling. Ari and I stepped over the threshold and into a dark space beyond.

It was a narrow cavern. As the door dropped shut behind us, Ari and I shone our torches over the walls. They did seem to have been cut, and a series of niches ran along either wall. In some of the niches were little bowls. Above the niches, the stone was often stained black.

"Oil lamps," observed Ari.

"Look." I pointed. Now that our eyes were getting used to the dark, we could see a dim bluish light. We made for it.

The man-made passageway soon gave way to walls of living rock, twisted into fantastic shapes. The way would narrow so that we had to squeeze sideways, or the roof would drop so that we would have to crawl. Pillars of rock rose on either hand, sometimes wound about with intricate shapes like a dripping candle.

All the time, the blue light ahead of us grew in strength.

Minutes seemed to stretch into hours in that cramped, weird place. I consulted my wristwatch, but I couldn't remember when we had started our journey. The evening, I saw, was well advanced, and I suddenly noticed a grumbling in my stomach.

"Ari," I said, "would you like some salami and cheese?"

"Very much," she replied, turning around as I reached into my backpack. We prayed grace, then resumed our journey, munching on the food as we went.

Ari stopped to examine something closely. When I got close to her, I saw that there was a patch of phosphorescent lichen on the wall, shining faintly with blue.

"There must be more of it than that, though," I said. "There's more light that way."

We scrambled over great steps of rock, slithered down stone ramps, and wriggled around columns of rock that might have been the width of a man's waist.

"I can't remember the difference," I grumbled, "between a stalactite and a stalagmite."

"A stalactite hangs down from the roof," said Ari, "and a stalagmite grows up from the floor."

"How do you remember that?" I inquired.

"A stala*ctite* clings *tight* to the roof," she replied. "Someday, the stalag*mite might* reach it."

For a moment, we were both able to stand upright, and the blue light was almost strong enough that we could do away with the torches. Ari unshouldered her backpack, took out a bundle and unrolled it. It was a jacket. True enough, it was getting cold down there, and it seemed colder because we were both still damp from the flooded chambers. As she bent over the backpack to buckle it up, something slipped out of the neck of her shirt and hung there for a moment. It flashed in the blue light like a diamond. But I didn't have a chance to ask about it, for she had shouldered the backpack and struck off towards the blue light.

"Can you hear something?" I asked.

She cocked her head on one side. "It sounds like running water."

We found ourselves at the bottom of a flight of steps that had been cut into the rock. The middle was worn slightly, but otherwise they were of a tremendously regular shape. Now the sound of water

148

was quite loud as it echoed and re-echoed from the walls.

Slowly, we mounted the steps. We could see that there was a wide and open space at the top, and the blue light was actually bright up there. I flicked off my torch.

At last, we reached the top of the steps and gazed into the wide cavern beyond.

It was an almost perfectly circular space, and vast. The light came from more of the phosphorescent lichen that covered the walls of the cavern in patches. Around the edge of the cavern were thousands upon thousands of mighty stalagmites and stalactites. Nestling behind them were houses—we could see doors and windows, flat roofs, balconies, pavements, pillars that looked like street lamps. It was a small underground city.

Almost all the middle space of the cavern was an underground lake. It was fed by a waterfall at the far end of the cavern: the water erupted from a spout twenty feet up the rock-face, hitting the surface in a foaming mass. At each of the compass-points a perfectly straight path led from the shore to the centre of the lake, where they formed a cross. At the intersection was a spiral of green copper, rotating constantly. Buckets seemed to be suspended from it, and they dipped into the waters of the lake, and then rose up the spiral and vanished from sight in the ceiling.

149

"Great Scott!" I exclaimed. "It's an Archimedes Screw!" Ari looked at me with a question in her eyes. "Inside that copper column," I explained, "is a helical surface surrounding a central shaft." Another question in her eyes. "It's a great big screw-thread. As it turns, it carries water up it to the top of the column. They were used in ancient Egypt for irrigation. Archimedes got the credit for inventing them, though they probably existed before his lifetime— well, they certainly did." I pointed. "There's one seventeen hundred years older than Archimedes." I wandered to the shore of the lake and looked up. At the top of the Archimedes Screw was a wide circular hole in the cavern roof, and I could see chutes emanating from it like the main strands in a spider's web. Water seemed to be splashing from the top of the screw and pouring off down the chutes. "We were wondering where Thera's fresh water came from," I said; "it comes from here."

"These buildings!" said Ari, turning away from that marvel of engineering to examine a mere house. She stepped through the door, and I saw her torch-light shining through the window. I went inside to join her.

It was a whole house, complete and perfectly preserved. We wandered from room to room, marveling at the paintings on the walls. The ancient Therans had depicted their everyday lives on those walls. We saw women sitting at spinning wheels or

150

eating at table; fishermen with nets; boys and girls leaping over the backs of bulls in arenas; and we saw a profusion of wildlife: dolphins, birds, monkeys. On one wall was a depiction of the minotaur. In another room was a stone bowl, directly under a spout that came through the wall. It had a stopper in the top, and when Ari pulled on the stopper, water gushed from the spout into the bowl. She stooped and let the water run into her mouth, then replaced the stopper, cutting off the free flow.

"It's fresh, all right," she said. "But how did they get fresh water?" There was a window outside, and she stood in the frame for a moment, contemplating the Archimedes Screw.

I cleared my throat. "I couldn't help noticing," I said hesitantly, "what you're wearing around your neck."

She half-turned so that her profile was framed by the window. "I didn't wear it for a long time," she said. "After you . . . left Rio, I buried it deep in one of my suitcases and didn't look at it for two years. I thought, 'Maybe McCracken isn't the man for me.'"

"But you're wearing it now," I pointed out.

"I found it when I got aboard the LS3. Silly me, I was using one of the suitcases I used in Rio. And there it was, looking like it did when you first gave it me."

"Ari, I—"

"Don't, Mac," she interrupted. "I know what you're going to say. But I believe you're wrong. We either love, or we fear. You chose fear. And when you hear about God's plan for you, it's always going to be wrong to choose fear instead of love and danger and risk."

At that moment, against all expectations, we heard the sound of a human voice from outside in the cavern. "Herr Sikorsky! Herr McCracken! Fraulein Bell!" cried the voice.

"That's Fritz," said Ari, and we both dashed outside.

Fritz saw us at once and hurried up to us. "Herr McCracken, Fraulein Bell!" he sobbed. "So glad I am to see you here! You must come at once—*schnell*! Please!"

"What's wrong, Fritz?" asked Ari.

"It is the Baron—he is in terrible danger."

We hurried along the side of the lake towards the far side. "What's happening, Fritz?" I asked.

"The Baron—by a huge creature he is seized."

"A creature?" I thumbed back the safety on my revolver. "What kind of creature?"

"I cannot describe, Herr McCracken," said Fritz, urging us on with frantic gestures. "It is like a man shaped, but it have huge head, with horns."

"Horns?"

"*Ja*, horns," said Fritz. "But it is not like a man either—more like *Affe*."

"An ape?"

"*Ja*, it is covered all over with hair."

We had reached the far side of the lake, and now dashed towards the waterfall. In the rock below it was a doorway with roughly-hewn lintels.

"Through there?" Fritz nodded vigorously. I raised my revolver, switched on my electric torch, and stepped towards the doorway.

"Mac!" said Ari sharply. I turned. "Think. The creature is shaped like a man, but with a large, horned head."

"Yes?"

She turned to Fritz. "Describe the shape of the creature's head," she said.

"It is not a man's head. It is more like . . . like . . . *ein Stier*."

"A bull?" Fritz nodded, and Ari and I looked at one another. "A minotaur?" we said together.

"And that," said Ari, stepping forward and indicating the doorway, "is its labyrinth."

CHAPTER 13
LABYRINTHS AND LAVA

I knew the legend of the minotaur. Who hasn't read that chilling tale as a child? I even had Ariadne with me. And like every good adventurer, I had a ball of string in my backpack. I took it out, wrapped it around a stalagmite and, unspooling it as I went, plunged into the darkness beyond the doorway, Ari and Fritz close at my heels.

The passageway was cut roughly from stone, and almost immediately it divided into three.

"Which way did he go, Fritz?" asked Ari, her voice strangely muffled in the close confines. Fritz shrugged and shook his head. But I shone my torch over the ground, and saw that the dirt had been recently disturbed in the mouth of the right-hand passage.

"I think it's this way," I said; and we went on, unreeling the string as we walked.

Before too long, we had another choice, when our passageway intersected with another perpendicular to it. The dirt here was hard-packed, and I could see no evidence of a disturbance.

"Just choose a direction," suggested Ari.

So I chose right. We walked on, the passage turning, turning again, doubling back on itself. As

154

cold as it had been out in the cave, it was hot and stuffy down here, and Ari pulled off her jacket. I don't mind the honest heat of machinery. You just roll up your sleeves and get to work. But this nasty, stuffy heat of the underground—it's like the grave.

"Uh-oh," I said, and all three of us came to a halt. A few yards ahead of us, the passageway was blocked by a cave-in. It was mostly soil, but I could see chunks of masonry that had given way.

"Do you think that was deliberate?" wondered Ari. "To throw us off?"

I looked closely at it. "No, this happened years ago—perhaps centuries ago. But we should have taken the left-hand passage."

We returned the way we had come. The passage turned and turned. For the most part, it was about four feet wide and seven feet in height, but at one point, it widened out into a gallery whose left-hand wall we couldn't see even with the beams of our torches. The path we followed, however, was still only three feet wide, with a drop-off on the left side. Shining my torch down it, I saw all sorts of rubbish gathered at the bottom of it: pieces of wood and pottery, and bones—lots and lots of bones. I remembered the tale of Theseus, and shuddered.

"Don't look," I advised Ari and Fritz; but my voice was loud in the gallery, and there was a consequence: a rustling, like the rustling of thousands of huge leaves over our heads. Without thinking about it, I flashed my torch overhead.

The whole ceiling of the gallery was moving. The light flashed over thousands of tiny eyes and teeth. Ari cried out in fright, and Fritz said, "*Mein Gott!*" We all ducked—just in time.

A cloud of bats descended from the ceiling and filled the air over our heads. They squeaked and shrieked as they went, and swooped low enough to brush the tops of our heads. My skin crawled. I actually like bats—some of them are even fair to look upon—but to have these unseen things gibbering inches over my head, their leather wings stirring the clammy air, their sharp little talons clutching down at me—well, that was not an experience I really wanted to repeat.

After a few moments, the deluge of bats subsided, and we were able to straighten up and proceed along our course. A few more paces brought us to a place where we were back in a narrow passageway again. Soon, we came to a junction where we paused because the dirt was disturbed in both directions; but we heard an unearthly growl, and followed that. Once, we passed through a small and empty chamber, scattered with rags and ancient bones. We didn't examine them, but went on.

A few more turns, and the string ran out. Ari took out hers and tied the two ends together, then we continued on our way.

Just when it seemed that we'd never reach the end of the labyrinth, the passage opened out into another wide cave.

This was somewhat smaller than the other cave, and lower too, but it also had a lake in its middle, though this lake was different. It was a lake of molten rock, and it cast a lurid light over the walls and roof. I remembered what the Baron had told us, that he knew where the Lake of Fire was, where the Therans stored their reserves of orichalcum.

In the middle of the lake was a stone structure, about twenty feet wide, a roof supported by two lines of Minoan columns. The roof was lit by light of a different colour, and I thought there might be a hole in the roof above it, through which shone light from outside. There was a jumbled collection of objects on the floor, objects I couldn't identify at this distance. A path led across the Lake of Fire to steps that ascended to the entrance of the structure. And there, outlined against the red glow of the lake, stood a terrible shape, resembling a man but stooped like an ape and with an oversized, horned head. It was the very picture of a fiend. Without thinking, I leveled my revolver, took aim, and fired. The creature staggered, and my second shot went wide. I saw it put down a burden it carried—the Baron either was dead or had fainted.

And then the minotaur came dashing towards me.

I had once been rushed by a bull elephant in West Africa, but then I had had an elephant gun, and an elephant was a known creature. This was nothing I'd ever seen before, or hoped to see ever again. I fired off four shots, and then the hammer clicked against the chamber with a hollow sound. Ari, I saw, was drawing her own gun. But the beast was on me, with the force of an express train. I had the impression of fiery, inhuman eyes and a pair of wide, dark nostrils, and then I was on my back, all the air expelled from my lungs.

I thought I would be dead soon. I wondered what it would be like to meet God. I wondered if I had any unconfessed sins on my conscience. I wished I could ask Ari—she would know what they were.

But another shot crashed out, and another, and another. The beast stood up, leaving me alone for the moment.

Another crash and a flash of light, and the beast took a step back. Still, it wasn't dead, but it was a little confused. It staggered back one pace, then another, a confused noise coming from its lips. Then it took a step a little too far, and howled, for it had stepped into the lake. With a bellow of pain, it threw up its arms and fell backwards. A fountain of molten rock flew up in the air, and the creature was gone.

"Mac!"

I rolled over and tried to push myself to my feet. My head was spinning, though, and I couldn't do it. Ari was at my side. I pulled myself to my feet.

"Thank you," I said. "I wonder what his beef was?"

"Let me steer you away from any more puns," said Ari.

At that moment, we heard another noise: the bellow of a creature, similar to the minotaur's bellow.

"Och, I knew it couldn't be the only one," I said grimly. "Come on, let's get the Baron."

The three of us set out along the path towards the island. It was a narrow path, and the lava lapped up towards our feet constantly. The heat was fantastic. I felt as if it was going to burn the flesh from my bones.

At last, we reached the island, and there was the Baron. I stooped and felt for a pulse. Ari had her water bottle at his lips. He stirred, and then his eyes opened.

"Herr McCracken?" he said weakly. "Fraulein Bell? *Wo bin ich?*"

"I don't know where we are," I said, "in the middle of the Lake of Fire, I think. But we have to get you back to the airship." I helped him to his feet.

It was at that moment that I noticed all the objects that were lying around on the floor of this building. I could see a hammer and tongs, some bellows (the leather was perished), and large, formless items that, upon closer examination, turned out to be moulds for a variety of different implements.

"This is their orichalcum smithy," I said. I turned slowly round, surveying the lake of lava. "So all this molten rock is orichalcum in its pure form," I said quietly. A globule of the lava jumped out of the lake and hit the ground just before my toes. I watched curiously as it cooled—very quickly, I thought. I prodded it with the end of my knife, but it was solid now and quite cool. "It cools quickly," I said, "so practically the only thing you can do with it is mould it into the right shape." I held the small piece up to the light. "If it's small, it's translucent, like a gemstone." I looked at another, larger lump of rock that had evidently come from the lake. "If it's thick, though, it's opaque, and looks like metal—like the plates you and Sikorsky saw riveted to the wall, Baron. Fascinating."

"Thanks for the science lesson, Mac," said Ari, "but we have to leave now."

But before we could move two steps onto the path, the lake lurched, and molten rock washed over the path. When it ebbed away, the path was gone and we were stranded in the middle of the Lake of Fire. We gazed at it in disbelief. The lava jumped up in little peaks like the waves of the sea, and heaved left and right under some terrible power. Ari said, "I can't believe it. That path has been there for four thousand years, and it gets washed away now, just when we need it."

"That's a little frustrating," I said. "Now how are we going to get out of here?"

Holding onto one of the columns, I leaned out over the lava and gazed up at the roof. Above it there was, as I had thought earlier, an opening through the rock, and pale light flooded down from it. Naturally, they would need a vent through which fumes could escape—it would be impossible to work in such an enclosed space for long. Safety regulations would strictly forbid it, I thought, smiling to myself.

I couldn't see anything through the hole in the roof, though. I explained what I had seen to the others. The Baron still seemed a little dazed and said nothing; Fritz looked fearful as he lamented. Ari said, "Right. So, do you have a plan?"

"Not yet," I answered. "What do we have in the backpacks?"

We hastily emptied them. Each contained food, a mess kit, a blanket, a coil of rope, extra rounds for the revolver, my collapsible ski poles, a mirror, and a first-aid kit.

"I think we can do something with these items," I said to myself.

"What?" asked Ari.

"You'll see."

I took the sticking-plasters out of the first-aid kit and taped the knives from the mess kits together so that they formed a cross. Then I pulled the ski pole into two pieces. One of them had a slightly wider diameter so the other would fit into it. I took the inner part, and fixed the crossed knives to one end. Then I rolled up some of the bandage and stuffed them down the inner section of the ski-pole, tamping them down with a fork-handle. I looked about on the floor, until I found a piece of orichalcum that would fit snugly into the ski-pole, and pressed that in as well. There was about an inch of space left in the ski-pole, and into this I poured the gunpowder from one of the bullets. Then I cut the primer from the bullet and fixed it into the end of the ski-pole. Finally, I slotted them back together, wiggling them around to loosen the fit a little, whilst it remained pretty snug. Then I tied the rope to the inner section of the ski-pole, just below the crossed knives.

Then I handed the completed contraption to Ari. "Pass that to me when I'm on the roof," I said.

"Hurry, Mac," said Ari. I looked where she was looking, and saw that the lava had actually crept up and was almost level with the floor of the workshop.

"Don't worry," I said, "we'll soon be out of here." I kissed her—it was my dramatic flair getting the better of me—and then shinned up one of the pillars to the roof. "I'll take that contraption now," I said, holding out my hand. Ari handed it up to me. I set

162

it down on the ceiling of the workshop. The light was blue on the upper sides of the knives, and crimson on the lower sides. The colours reminded me of the LS3, the first time I had seen her.

"St. Joseph," I said quietly, "give me a hand here, please." I crossed myself.

Then I raised the contraption a few inches and slammed it down on the roof of the workshop. The action struck the base of the ski-pole against the primer, and there was a terrific bang as the gunpowder ignited. The mini-explosion was magnified by the orichalcum stone, and the inner section of the ski-pole, under the force of the explosion, shot out of the outer section and flew high in the air. It sailed through the hole in the roof, and came to a rest somewhere above.

"Ha!" I cried with joy; I had improvised a mortar.

I pulled gently on the rope, until I found that the crossed knives caught on something. Then I dipped my head below the roof-line of the workshop.

"You can come up now," I said. "I have a rope."

One by one, they climbed up onto the roof. Ari was wide-eyed, and her jaw hung loose in amazement. "How did you do that?" she asked.

"When you're desperate, you find a way," I replied. "I'll go up first and secure the rope properly; you all come up after me, one at a time—send the Baron, then Fritz. You last, Ari." I know that sounds unchivalrous, but I reckoned that Ari would be the better climber, and keep a cooler head than either of the others. She would be able to get up the rope quickly if the temple started collapsing.

I grabbed the rope and hauled myself up. Unprotected now by the roof of the workshop, I felt a tremendous blast of heat as I worked my way up. But the distance was not great, and I was soon rolling away from the edge into another cavern. The place was bright, and I could hear running water. It was hot from the lava below, and full of steam. I found my makeshift grappling hook, and tied the rope to a handy stalagmite. Then I called down to the others that the rope was secure.

Fritz was the first up. He was actually much faster than I had imagined—the little fellow seemed to be full of surprises. Then the Baron started up, muttering to himself in German. At first, he couldn't pull his own weight up the rope. Ari showed him how to grip it with his knees, and held the bottom end taut for him. But still, his progress was laboursome.

From my angle, I could see that one of the particularly high waves of lava had lapped up onto the temple floor. It smoked for a moment, then its angry crimson died to a dull brown.

"Baron, try to be a little quicker!" I called. "The lava is getting higher."

"My arms—they hurt," he replied, looking up. Once again, his eyes were hidden by his spectacles. "When a minotaur you has mauled, you may criticize me."

"I'm going to pull on you a little," I warned him, and hauled on the rope. It was slow going at first—the Baron was not a slim man—but once Fritz lent a hand, the going was quicker. The Baron scrambled up and joined us. I let down the rope to Ari, and she climbed swiftly up it. A moment after she had seized the rope, one of the columns supporting the workshop roof collapsed sideways into the lava with a great scarlet splash. The roof tumbled, bit by bit, into the seething lava. In about twenty seconds, it was all gone, as if it had never existed. I reflected for a brief moment on the sadness of the loss of all those smithing tools.

But then I saw something much more pressing: the end of the rope had touched the lava, and fire flashed up it.

"Give me your hand!" I shouted, holding it out. Ari grabbed me around the wrist and released the rope, just as the fire flashed along its length and it vanished into ashes. For a few moments, my muscles strained, but then I was able to haul Ari up enough so that she could grab the edge of the hole and pull herself through it. Fortunately, she wasn't as heavy as the Baron.

At last, we could take stock of our new sur-roundings. Above our heads was a great green bowl—it must have been fifteen or so yards in diam-eter. Into it, from all directions, poured water, from apertures in the wall all around it. Steam rose from the bowl, onto a great green concave surface above it. There the steam formed condensation, which poured off into a flume beyond it. The whole thing was happening very fast, so that water gushed down the flume and into a tunnel.

"What is this?" asked Ari.

"This," I said, rapping the green bowl with my knuckles—it was very hot, "is the Chalice of the Tides. The Therans talked of harnessing the power of the sea. I think they managed it."

"How?"

I held my fingers under the water pouring into the bowl. It tasted salty. Then I tried the water from the condensation. It was sweet.

"This is a desalination plant," I said. "At least, that's the term we use nowadays. It takes salt water, and by converting it to steam and then distilling that steam back into water, removes the salt. That's how the island gets its fresh water. Then there are the crystals we saw before in the ceiling of the dome that protected Thera when it was underwater. Between them, they explain how the jungle has remained alive. Plants need light and fresh water. The Ther-ans found a way of manufacturing both. This one

166

empties into the lake we saw earlier—the one with the city on its shores." I looked around. "I imagine that this isn't the only one of these—by itself, it wouldn't produce nearly enough fresh water for nearly two thousand square miles, which is approximately Thera's area."

"And now, *meine Freunde*," said the Baron's voice, "you will please to hand over the orichalcum."

Ari and I turned, and found that he had a Luger trained on us.

CHAPTER 14
DOUBLING BACK

A few moments of silence passed while Ari and I contemplated the muzzle of the gun staring at us. Slightly behind the Baron, Fritz cringed, wringing his hands.

"*Nein, Mein Herr, nein!*" he said. "*Sie hat uns gerettet*—they saved us! *Nicht scheißen, bitte, nicht scheißen!*"

"Don't be stupid, Fritz!" the Baron barked back. "This is the reason why we came here. It is not now we can turn back."

"*Bitte, Mein Herr!*" said Fritz, pawing at his sleeve.

"Release me at once, Fritz, or you also I shall shoot!"

Fritz released him and stepped backwards, averting his eyes from us.

The Baron spoke almost apologetically. "You must excuse Fritz, Herr McCracken, Fraulein Bell. He is very stupid, and very weak. When to Germany I return, I believe I will employ a new servant."

Behind him, Fritz cringed to hear these words, but the Baron didn't notice. He just advanced a few steps and held out his hand. "And now the orichalcum, if you please."

"I don't have it," I replied.

The Baron remained perfectly still for a count of three. "Please, I beg of you, Herr McCracken, do not try to deceive me. I shall have no qualms about shooting dead you and Fraulein Bell, and then I can from your bodies take whatever I please."

"No, I mean it, Baron. I don't have the orichalcum stones. You know that the door will only open when those stones are in place. I had to leave them there so that we could get out again. You left them there too."

The Baron blinked. "You are an engineer, Herr McCracken. I had thought you would find a way to keep the door open whilst removing the stones. Perhaps I had overestimated your skills. But I feel confident that you will find a way now."

I took a step forward, and stuck my chest out at him. "I think you ought to just shoot me and have done with it all, Baron. Go ahead—fire."

The Baron chuckled with a kind of grim merriment. "Most amusing theatricals, Herr McCracken. Is your performance solely designed to impress Fraulein Bell? I could shoot you, of course. But I need you to retrieve the orichalcum stones. However, I think you would probably feel a little different if I shot Fraulein Bell."

With that, he reached out a lightning-quick hand and seized Ariadne. He pulled her close to him, holding her by the throat, and thrust the muz-

169

zle of the gun against her temple. I took a step towards him, my blood boiling with rage, but I saw his finger tighten on the trigger, and couldn't get a step closer.

"And now, Herr McCracken, the orichalcum stones you will retrieve. Fritz!" Fritz shuffled up. "Remove the revolver from Fraulein Bell's holster, and tie her hands and feet. And, Fritz?"

"*Ja, Mein Herr?*"

"*I* will check the knots," the Baron insisted.

"*Jawohl, Mein Herr,*" said Fritz; and I saw that he wept as he did it.

"I suggest, Herr McCracken, that you begin at once. If I have not the orichalcum stones in two hours, Fraulein Bell I will shoot."

I called him a name that shouldn't really be printed, and turned to go, but he called me back. "Herr McCracken—your backpack, your knife, and your revolver. You will leave them here."

Muttering more unprintable words, I laid the items on the floor. Ari was all trussed up now. Her wrists were white around the knots, and she moved awkwardly because of the ropes around her ankles. The Baron set her down on the floor by a large boulder.

"What do you think you're going to gain by this, Baron?" I demanded.

The Baron chuckled. "Oh, I imagine you can make a shrewd guess, Herr McCracken," he said.

Ari wriggled, striving against her bonds, but she couldn't move. "The Kaiser will, I am sure, reward me very greatly for providing his army with a power source that will make it invincible. War is coming, Herr McCracken. You have said it yourself. The side will win which is the best prepared."

"That's absurd," I said. "Orichalcum doesn't belong you, or to Germany—it belongs to the world."

"Orichalcum, Herr McCracken, belongs to whoever can possess it."

"You're insane," I told him, bitterly.

"Insane?" The Baron took an aggressive step forward, waving the gun before him. "What an old-fashioned Catholic point of view you adopt, Herr McCracken!" He whipped off his glasses, so that his eyes appeared to be two points of red light. "The Middle Ages are over and dead," he went on. "We live in a new world, a world of technology and fantastic power—the power to create and the power to destroy. Is that insane? I hardly think so. On the contrary, it is beautiful. Power untrammeled by conscience is a thing of beauty. Is it insane to see the German race running every government in the world? We do it better than everyone else. The Italians cannot run Italy, the French cannot run France—that is what is absurd, Herr McCracken. The German race *will* run the world better than anyone else. We have the ability to do it, we have the

171

right to do it and, with the orichalcum, we will have the power to do it. I ask you, Herr McCracken, how is that insane?"

"Well, I suppose if you have to ask the question, I can't explain it to you," I replied.

"Precisely, Herr McCracken," replied the Baron. "Perhaps now, at last, you begin to see the sublime beauty of this plan." Now his eyes had softened, and he looked on me almost as a father would his son. "Perhaps you are not beyond redemption, Herr McCracken. Perhaps you, although you are not Prussian, can have a part in our plans. There is room within them for a man of your talents and creativity." He glanced over his shoulder. Ari was still struggling against her bonds. "Perhaps a place for Fraulein Bell too. The Americans are a degenerate race, but the breed will improve if mixed with nobler blood."

"And Jaubert? Sikorsky?"

"There can be no hope for the French," snapped the Baron, "or for the Russians. They will be eliminated." He held up a clenched fist towards me. "Come with me, Herr McCracken. You and I can bring this new master-plan for the human race to fruition. A new era is dawning. Things will not fall apart, the centre will hold, and the centre will be Berlin!"

"This is the same logic the wolf uses to justify eating the sheep," I countered. "It's the fanatical log-

172

ic of every tyrant for centuries. And you know how they all finish up, Baron—lying in a ditch somewhere, with a bullet through their brains. It doesn't have to be this way. God won't bless Germany if she insists on dominating rather than leading in love and by example."

"How quaint and old-fashioned your Catholic beliefs are, Herr McCracken," rejoined the Baron. "When you think about my offer, you will see the wisdom of it. You have said it well: there are wolves and there are sheep in this new world of ours. If you wish to survive, you must choose to be a wolf."

"You can choose to be a wolf if you like," I answered, "but sooner or later, you'll have to face the shepherd."

"I have no fear of shepherds, Herr McCracken," said the Baron. He lifted the Luger. "This is more powerful than a crook. You refuse to join me, then?"

"I don't work with evil geniuses," I said firmly.

The Baron gave a small sigh. "It is most regrettable," he said and, taking a watch from his pocket and flipping its lid, added, "You have two hours, Herr McCracken."

"It took more than two hours to get here, Helleher-Stauffen," I said. "I need more time."

"And yet, I think you will not have it, Herr McCracken." He returned the watch to his pocket. "You had better hurry." And he smiled at me with an air of infuriating smugness.

173

I stepped over to Ari and bent down before her. The Baron flinched and raised his gun, but I simply reached behind her neck and slipped what was around it over her head. The diamond ring flashed in the light. I took the engagement ring I had given her in Rio off the chain-pump and put it on her finger.

"When I get back," I said, "I'll be ready. We'll start facing all the dangers together. If you agree, that is."

"Oh, I agree," said Ari, smiling although she was in pain from the tightness of her bonds. She held up her bound wrists. "In fact, I'd argue that we've already begun sharing the dangers. But, Mac, don't go. It's not worth it—if he shoots me, that's only one life. What's that to the millions that would be lost in a great war?"

"That's good logic, Ari," I said, standing up, "but it's bad theology. I'd better be going. Pray for me."

With that, I turned and dived into the water that was pouring down the flume.

For what seemed a very long time, I plunged through the darkness and tepid water. I held my hands straight out in front of me, fearing lest I should strike an obstacle concealed by the utter darkness. But the flume went more or less straight, though it wavered a bit, and it was unobstructed. Part of the way down, my hand struck against something, a knob or handle that projected from the side, and I realized that the ancient engineer had designed the flume with hand-holds for ease of maintenance.

What a genius!

Then, abruptly, I shot out into mid-air and landed with a great splash in the middle of a lake. It was quite a deep lake, and I described a graceful underwater arc before I began to rise. Breaking the surface some yards from the edge, I saw that I was in the cave with the Archimedes Screw. I struck out for the nearest path and clambered up onto it. Dripping as I went, I ran along the path, past the Screw, and towards the far side of the cavern.

It was crazy, I thought, the whole thing was crazy. How would the Baron get out? There was no way out through the Lake of Fire. He would have to come the same way as I was going now, and that meant down the flume. He would not be able to ensure my or Ari's behaviour if he let us out of his sight. There was only one thing he could do.

I didn't like to think about that.

There had to be something I could do. Perhaps the LS3 would be waiting for me at the Temple of the Minotaur, and I could get Sikorsky's help, or a pistol, or both. Perhaps Jaubert would be able to help.

But I couldn't rely on their help. They were, I realized, two of the most dependable chaps I had ever met, but the chances were good they wouldn't be there. They were most likely still at the Temple of Ariadne.

I dashed on, snaking through the cramped spaces of the tunnels. It was freezing cold, and my soaked clothes made it worse. How much time had passed? I wondered. I shone my torch on my wrist. About fifteen minutes, I estimated. Sharp spurs of rock plucked at my clothing, low overhangs struck me on the head, but I didn't have time to nurse my wounds. I just ran on, a sharp pain beginning to claw through my side.

I don't know how the time passed, because I didn't dare pause to look at my watch again. I just kept going on. Always in the front of my thoughts was the image of Ari—my wife-to-be—tied up and cast against that boulder, the Baron crouching over her with the Luger in his hand.

Now I couldn't resist. I paused, flashed the light onto my watch. The torch's light was getting brown. I knew there were batteries in my backpack—way back there. I peered closely at the watch face.

Almost an hour had passed.

I went on.

And straight away, I found myself in a wider passage, cut by the hands of men, with a flat wall in front of me.

I realized with a shock that I didn't know how to open the door from this side, and stood in dreadful perplexity before the blank wall.

There must be a clue somewhere, I thought desperately, running my hands over the featureless surface.

Then my eyes fell upon a simple lever to the right of the door. I pressed it down, and with a reluctant groan, the door slid up into the ceiling. I passed under it, and it closed behind me.

The water in the chamber was up to my knees now, and I could hear the water turbine churning away in the antechamber. I pressed on the door, and it opened smoothly for me.

What I needed, I thought, was something to brace the door. I could see nothing that would do—nothing except the water turbine. That would have to do. I stooped over it and switched it off. The motor died, and the runner slowed to a stop. Silence fell upon the little antechamber as I disconnected the hose from the back of the turbine and slid my hands underneath it. It seemed heavier and more cumbersome than I remembered, but I recalled that the last time I had carried one, I had had Ari's help. I staggered over to the doorway and set the turbine down in it. Then I extracted the orichalcum stones. Instantly, the door slammed on the water turbine with a horrid crunching noise. I leaped through the gap, and pocketed the fire stones.

The sliding door ahead of me was still closed, and the water was deep. Moving my torch between the wall and the floor, I stepped this way and that, pressing firmly with my toes to be sure each tile was properly depressed. I felt as if I could hear my watch ticking away, ticking and ticking and ticking, louder and ever louder, as the seconds and minutes passed towards Ari's doom.

The door slid up and I rushed through. Soon, I was out among the stalagmites and stalactites again. I ran and dodged and rolled, but still it seemed that an interminable amount of time passed before I emerged into the cavern and saw the Archimedes Screw ahead of me.

The tough part was going to be getting back up the flume, since going again through the labyrinth and across the Lake of Fire was unthinkable. I threw off my boots and socks to get a better grip, and climbed up the rock-face to where the water vented into the lake. I raised myself up level with the mouth of the flume, and the water dashed against my face like an avalanche of wet bricks. For a few seconds, I could do nothing but hold on, as the water threatened to throw me off and back into the lake any second. But then I braced myself, and pulled my weight up into the mouth of the flume. Water fountained up past my head and shoulders, and for a few seconds I could not breathe. I reached into the flume with my hands, and found one of the hand-holds. I heaved myself up and pushed with my feet, and gained a few inches. Still, the water gushed into my face. I pulled and pushed, and at last forced my hips past the flume's mouth. I raised my head above the water a few seconds, and gulped down some sweet breaths of air. Then I rotated myself onto my stomach, and began my climb. The hand- and foot-holds helped, but I was crawling against the flow of the water, and it was agonizingly slow going. At any moment, I thought, the water would wash me from the flume and propel me down it and back into the lake. And I had not a moment to lose. I couldn't consult my watch, but I knew that it must have been almost two hours at least at this point. If Ari wasn't already dead, she soon would be.

Ari dead. The thought gripped me right in the stomach. The last two years without her had been bitter, I realized, but I had pushed my loneliness deep down inside me, where I could ignore it, and had contented myself with dangerous adventures to avoid thinking about her. To lose her now would be unthinkable. "God," I prayed, "if You save Ari now, I promise I'll never argue with You about marrying her again."

Moments later, my head emerged from the water, and there I was beneath the great copper bowl once more. Ari was still tied up against the boulder, and the Baron stood beside her, the Luger still in his hand. Seeing me, he smiled and advanced towards me.

"Ah, Herr McCracken, there you are!" he crowed, taking out his watch and flipping it open.

179

"We were beginning to wonder where you were." He studied the watch face closely. "One hour, fifty-six minutes, and thirty-eight seconds." He looked directly at me as he tucked the watch back in his pocket. "Well, they say the secret of good comedy is timing." He held out his hand. "And now you will kindly hand over the orichalcum," he said, his smile not altering by one iota.

CHAPTER 15
PISTOLS AT DAWN

I looked down at the Baron's pudgy hand, and faced defeat for the first time in . . . well, longer than I could remember. Grimacing as I did so, I took the fire stones out of my pocket, and plunked them down in the palm of his hand. They clicked together as he rattled them in his fist.

"That's a pretty small amount of orichalcum to be happy with, Baron," I observed. "It looks like you've dropped your sights a bit. You shoot for the Moon, but before long, you're happy just zapping your neighbour. Well, that's how evil works."

"*Jawohl*, Herr McCracken," replied the Baron. "Our neighbours happen to be Belgium, France, and Russia. I look forward much to the zapping, as you put it. And if Imperial Germany demands more orichalcum, I know where to find it—thanks to you and our friends, Herr McCracken."

Chuckling, he closed his fingers smugly over the gems and looked over his shoulder. "Fritz, untie Fraulein Bell's legs, and keep your gun trained on her. This way, if you please, Herr McCracken."

He waved the Luger towards the back of the cave. I went on ahead of him. As we walked, the

Baron talked endlessly. Villainy seemed to have made him loquacious.

"You see, Herr McCracken, you are not the only . . . what is the English word for *Forscher*? *Jaeger*?"

"*Explorer*, Mein Herr," suggested Fritz.

"*Sehr gut*, Fritz," replied the Baron. "You are not the only explorer in this party, Herr McCracken. While Fraulein Bell was—ahem—resting, Fritz conducted his own exploration, and found something very surprising indeed."

"I'm dying to find out."

The Baron chuckled. "Oh, you are very funny, Herr McCracken. Your wit—something for which you will be remembered, no doubt. Dying to find out—you are closer to the truth than perhaps you think."

He went on chuckling for a few moments. In the meantime, our torches picked out a spiral staircase ahead of us. Fritz went first, lamenting in German as he did so. Then went Ari, then myself, and then the Baron, the Luger's muzzle trained on the small of my back.

"Fritz, *die Klappe halten*!" snapped the Baron. Fritz dutifully hushed at once, but I thought I could still hear him faintly.

The yellow pools of torch-light went up and up and up, and before too long I could hear the Baron puffing away as he climbed. But then some pale light appeared ahead of us, and I thought I could smell something sweet—the open air!

Moments later, we all emerged onto a flat, rocky landscape, roughly circular, high up in the air, and about a mile wide. We had arrived at the top of Russian's Folly. The shadows cast by the ruins were dark, sharp, and long, and they stretched out into the west, so I knew it was early morning.

"Ah!" cried the Baron. "And here is the LS3. This has been a morning of good timings!"

Sure enough, the airship was approaching from the east. The rising sun spilled along its slender lines, so that its outline appeared to be composed of fire.

"Walk, Herr McCracken," ordered the Baron. "You also, Fraulein Bell."

Out of the side of her mouth, Ari said, "Mac, I just wanted you to know that, you remember all those rotten things I said about you?"

"Yes?"

"Well, I didn't mean most of them."

"Which ones *did* you mean?" I asked.

"Well, the one about you being ignorant and having the manners of a wild boar. I meant those, at least at the time."

"But not the others?" I said.

"Actually the one about you smelling like a zoo on a hot day. I meant that one too."

"Well, it was a hot day," I said. "But not the others?"

"There were probably others too. But most of them I didn't mean."

"I'm glad you can be so honest, when we're facing almost certain death," I remarked.

"It's the best time to be honest, especially with the man who's going to be your husband. I mean, any time now we're going to face—"

"Halt!" barked the Baron, and we stopped. Right at the edge of the Folly. The ground was a very long way down. "And now, Herr McCracken, Fraulein Bell," he went on placidly, "as much as I have enjoyed your company, you will jump."

I peered over the edge and nudged a stone with my toe. It fell a little way, bounced off the side of the cliff, and continued falling, and falling, until I couldn't see it any more. I reached out and took Ariadne's hand.

"Ari," I said, "remember all those nice things I said about you?"

"There were a few," she admitted.

"Well, I meant to say more."

But before we could jump, the LS3 descended right in front of us. I could see Sikorsky at the controls, and Jaubert in the door of the gondola. Something was in his hands. It looked like a drinking horn, with wings on the sides, and a red gem set into its rim.

"Ari, get down!" I shouted.

We both dived flat on the rocky ground. As we did so, wind like a hurricane roared over our heads. I heard the Baron cry out and, looking over my shoulder, I saw him blown over backwards. He hit the ground and the Luger went flying from his hand.

The Therans had learned to control the air too, it seemed.

Jaubert pushed the rope ladder out of the gondola door, and Ari grabbed a rung and pulled herself up. Meanwhile, the wind had ceased.

When Ari was far enough up the rope ladder, I seized it and began my own ascent. Ari had disappeared inside, and I was nearly at the top, when I felt something grab my ankle. I looked down. The Baron was below me, his eyes afire. I shook my foot out of his grip, and felt it connect with something. The Baron grunted.

"Jaubert, let's get out of here!" I shouted.

Jaubert turned his head and cried out, "Vasili, *allez vite*! Ah—let us go!"

The airship began to turn away, just as I was able to scramble into the gondola. But the Baron wasn't far behind me, and in a moment, he was on his feet. He looked about himself like a trapped animal, for all three of us stood there waiting for the fight. But he didn't offer one. Instead, he dashed off up the steps to the upper deck.

"He has gone for weapons!" said Jaubert.

185

"Fraulein Bell!" cried a voice, "Herr McCracken, *helft mir*! Help me!"

Fritz's face was framed in the doorway. Ari stooped to help him, while I dashed after the Baron.

I was totally unarmed, so I approached the armoury cautiously, flat against the wall and in a crouch. The door was ajar. I could see a rack of shotguns and rifles inside, but it was a small room, and so I knew the Baron was not in it. Looking up, I saw that a trapdoor in the ceiling of the armoury was open. I took a couple of service revolvers, noting that several Lugers were missing from the drawer, and jumped up to grab the edge of the opening. In a moment, I had pulled myself through, dropping immediately to a crouch.

I was in the envelope of the airship itself. It seemed like a vast space, for all that it was mostly filled by the three massive hydrogen ballonets. I could see the aluminium ribs that stretched the cotton and linen skin of the envelope and helped the envelope retain its shape. I could see the gantries that ran along the inside of the skin and crossed right to left between the ballonets, where a maintenance crew could service those vital objects. Light came from halogen floodlights placed at regular intervals along the gantries.

In a moment, Ari and Fritz had joined me.

"What does that say?" I asked.

A lever protruded from the floor, beside which was a sign, which read, NOTFALL. ERHÖHEN HEBEL GONDEL LÖSEN.

"It says, *Raise lever to release gondola*," whispered Fritz. "I cannot tell what is *Notfall*."

"*Emergency*," suggested Ari. "Where's the Baron?"

Jaubert put his head through the trapdoor. "What is happening, Monsieur McCracken?" he asked.

"Tell Vasili to get the ship down as close to sealevel as he can," I said. Raising myself to my feet, I called out, "It's all over, Baron. You can't escape. Come peacefully, and I'll make sure you get a fair trial."

There came a chuckle from nearby, but I couldn't see the Baron himself. "But I have done nothing wrong, Herr McCracken. For what would anyone try me?"

That was puzzling, for a moment. He hadn't killed anyone, stolen anything, or started a war—yet. "How about multiple attempted murders?" I suggested.

He chuckled again—it was getting infuriatingly repetitive. "That is hardly anything you could prove, Herr McCracken. You would have to find a very good lawyer indeed, I think."

I tried a different approach. "Hand me the fire stones," I said, putting as much command into my voice as I could summon.

"*Ja, sehr gut*, Herr McCracken," said the Baron, and he rose from his hiding place nearby. One of the tungsten lights picked him out, like a spotlight in a theatre. "And hand over to His Majesty's Government of Britain the advantage over Imperial Germany? I think not." His eyes focused on Fritz. "Fritz, *kommen Sie hier*!" he said harshly. "Remember where are your wife and children!"

"Excuse me, *Herr und Fraulein*," said Fritz, squeezing past us to join his master. His face was a picture of misery. "And now, Herr McCracken and Fraulein Bell, for you it really is the end." He raised the Luger in his right hand. In his left, he held one of the fire stones, turning it and turning it endlessly between his fingers.

"You won't shoot us here," I countered, "with all this flammable gas around. Hydrogen explodes with a spark—and there's a lot of it here." My hand was on the lever that released the gondola.

"Actually, Herr McCracken, I think I will." He leveled the Luger at me. "From here, I will hit nothing important. I might puncture the side of the gondola, but that can always be patched." His finger tensed on the trigger. But then he lowered the gun. "Or, better still," he said, switching the fire stone to his right hand, "I shall use this. The poetic justice of killing you with the fire stone is—how is the English?—too good to miss."

The Baron held up the orichalcum gem so that light from one of the halogen lamps passed through it. I could see the fire light up in the gem's heart; in less than a second, it would concentrate the light and flash out towards me.

"*Nein, Mein Herr!*" shouted Fritz, leaping out and standing directly between the Baron and us. He had something in his hand, which I could see because he held it behind his back: one of the mirrors from my backpack, or from Ari's.

"What is this, Fritz?" demanded the Baron, lowering the stone as he drew himself up in all his Prussian pride. "Rebellion?"

"Do not kill them, Mein Herr," begged Fritz.

"I will," replied the Baron. "And it seems that I must kill you first. *Auf wiedersehen*, Fritz."

He held up the fire stone again, and the beam of red light leaped out. Fritz ducked, and held up the mirror to deflect the beam. It bounced right off, searing past the Baron's shoulder and boring a black hole into one of the hydrogen ballonets above him.

"Fritz, you fool!" shrieked the Baron.

Ari grabbed Fritz and dragged him towards us. I hauled on the lever. Wind rushed in among us, and light spilled in from outside.

The gondola sailed through the air. I had that horrid feeling of my stomach flying up above my head, that feeling you always get when you jump from a high place. Wind flew through our hair as we gripped the gondola for life. Fritz was with us, though Jaubert had gone below. Ahead of us was the wide, shimmering blue sheet of the Mediterranean.

Above us was a great yellow flower, that grew and grew with a roar until it seemed to fill the sky. The orichalcum fire had touched off the hydrogen.

Then the gondola hit the sea, and water flew upwards in all directions.

The last shreds of the LS3's envelope floated towards the earth, trailing smoke behind them. The great flame that had destroyed it still shimmered for a moment, rising through the air towards the clouds.

"Prepare to abandon ship!" I said urgently. "Fritz, do we have any lifeboats or jackets?"

"*Nein*, Herr McCracken," replied Fritz, "but there is no need—the Baron designed the gondola so that it could behave as a ship, if necessary."

"Oh yes, I'd forgotten," I said.

The air was clear again. The LS3's envelope had vanished, as if it had never been there. Somewhere ahead of us was the mainland of Greece.

"Well," I said, dropping down to the deck below and making my way for'ard, "I suppose we'd better learn how to sail a ship."

As I said it, we all heard a hum from the engines fore and aft. A moment later, the propellers that had pulled us through the air were pushing us through the water, in the direction of the mainland.

Sikorsky gave us a quick glance as we entered the wheel-house. "That was a bit surprising, McCracken," he said.

"But *très magnifique!*" cried Jaubert. "We should do it again, Monsieur McCracken—we should find out how high we can drop the gondola without breaking it."

"I think I'd like to take things easy for a little while," I commented. Out of the corner of my eye, I noticed Fritz, his head hanging low. "Fritz," I said, "thanks for intervening like you did. If you're stuck for a job right now, I have need of a driver and cook."

Fritz looked up, his mouth widening into a broad smile. "*Jawohl, Mein Herr!*" he said brightly.

"Hey, it's Sunday, isn't it?" asked Ari. Stepping closer to Sikorsky, she said, "Step on it, Vasili. We might get to the mainland in time for Mass."

And we did.

CHAPTER 16
A DIPLOMATIC SOLUTION

Mister McCracken!" said the swarthy Greek mechanic, his white overalls smeared here and there with oil, "the plane—it arrive!"

Ari and I left our cups of coffee—strong, black, and sweet—and strode out of the little building to the runway outside. The sun shone brightly upon the aerodrome in Siteia, Crete. The sea was a darker stripe of blue beneath the dazzling blue of the sky.

We could hear it already—the sound of four hundred horsepower pulling nearly nine thousand pounds of metal, wood, fabric, and glass was pretty loud. It was Sikorsky's plane, the Knight, which looked like a tram-car sandwiched between two pairs of spindly wings.

The gondola of the LS3 was moored at the local marina, among the fishing-boats and yachts. Sikorsky believed that, given appropriate working facilities, he could construct a new envelope for it, and have a new LS3 ready and operational in a year. It was he and Jaubert who had taken a train up to the Ukraine and, by stages, brought the four-engined Knight down to Greece while Ari and I had been attempting to persuade the various ambassadors in

Athens to listen to us. After a couple of months' work, we had persuaded a small group of international ambassadors to fly over Thera in the Knight, and now they were on their way back to the aerodrome in Crete.

The Knight touched down, with a squeal of rubber. The pitch of the engine changed and the plane coasted to a halt. For a moment, the propellers spun silently, and then stopped as a couple of mechanics dashed up to take care of maintenance.

People started filing out of the plane: the ambassadors to Greece of Great Britain, the United States, France, and Russia, the Greek Foreign Secretary, and a dapper man in his mid-sixties whom not I but Ari had invited. Last of all came Sikorsky himself, pulling his flying helmet from his head. The Knight's total payload was seven people, which is why Ari and I had stayed on the ground.

The diplomats filed, chattering among themselves, into the waiting room. Sikorsky ambled over to us. His face was grim.

"Is very bad, McCracken," he said. "Thera—she disappear."

"We knew it would," I said. "Has it completely disappeared?"

"No trace of her at all," replied the Russian, loosening the top buttons on his flying jacket. "Just a few bits of island, like there are when first we arrive."

"So what did their highnesses decide?"

Sikorsky shrugged. "They tell me nothing," he said. "But they laugh and joke all the way there, and all the way back. I think they are very—what is word?—skeptical."

The three of us went into the waiting room. The diplomats were all gathered about the table. Our coffees had been cleared away. When I closed the door behind us, all eyes turned in our direction.

"Ah, McCracken," said the British ambassador, "how nice to see you again. Mr. Sikorsky, let me thank you very much, on behalf of myself and all my colleagues, for a most invigorating and intellectually stimulating ride in your aeroplane."

Sikorsky nodded in acknowledgement; Ari and I sat down at the table.

"So, gentlemen," I said, "what do you think?"

"Think?" said the British ambassador. He put a hand to his throat and adjusted his bowtie slightly. "About what?"

"About Thera," I insisted.

The British ambassador took a breath and laid his hands out flat on the table in front of him. "Mr. McCracken, I'm dreadfully afraid we saw nothing to indicate the presence of anything remotely connected with a hidden island and fantastic powers. Mr. Sikorsky was good enough to fly us over an island called Thera, or Santorini, as my colleague Mr. Aristotle calls it."

"It has always been an uninhabited island, containing a large number of ancient ruins," said Aristotle, "but there is a possibility of developing it for purposes of tourism."

"Other than that," said the British ambassador, "and the antiquarian interest, I don't see what His Majesty's Government can do here."

"But I told you about the orichalcum!"

"Yes, you did, Mr. McCracken, you certainly did. Unfortunately, by your own account, all three of these orichalcum stones were lost upon the death of the Baron von Helleher-Stauffen. I should add that, inquiring of the Imperial German Government the whereabouts of the good Baron, I was informed that he had died on a hunting expedition in East Prussia." The ambassador spread his hands. "There you go, I'm afraid. The known facts don't square up with your account."

"Look," I said, "I have a sizeable part of an airship floating in the local marina, and a very nice Daimler outside that used to belong to Baron von Helleher-Stauffen."

"But since I have been reliably informed that the person you met was *not* the Baron von Helleher-Stauffen, then I'd say that you come out of this business with a very nice Daimler and an airship to your credit."

"You can't buy me off with a motor-car," I said. "When war comes, orichalcum could significantly tip the balance of power." I struggled to think of a way I could make a diplomat understand. "From a position of power, you could negotiate a peace that would be to the benefit of Britain and her allies."

"I am well aware of the diplomatic implications of such a weapon, should it exist," replied the ambassador, "but I'm afraid I remain unconvinced, and since I am the principle means of communicating with His Majesty's Government in Whitehall, I think my opinion may well carry the day with the king, God bless him."

"But at least you could go down there and have a look!" I insisted.

"Goodness gracious me!" the ambassador exploded. "Me, go down there, under the sea! What a preposterous idea!"

"Not you personally," I said, frustrated at being so deliberately misunderstood, "but someone representing all your governments."

"Mr. McCracken," put in the American ambassador, "given the powers you attribute to this stone, don't you realize that simply diving for it could be in itself considered an act of war?"

The British ambassador leaned close and dropped his voice to a whisper. "Mr. McCracken," he said, "it is tremendously important to persuade the royal government in Athens to join the war, if there is to be a war, on our side; we can't go fishing for super-weapons in their territorial waters and expect a positive response from them. The answer is, and must be, no." He turned to his colleagues. "Gentlemen, I believe we might make lunch in Heraklion, if we hurry."

Amid mumbling, hand-shakings, and polite comments I couldn't understand, the ambassadors left. Sitting alone at the table was the dapper gentleman Ari had invited.

Sikorsky cast a bitter look about the room. "The Knight, she need my attention," he said, and left.

The gentleman at the table stood up and held out his hand to me. "Mr. McCracken, I believe we haven't been introduced," he said. "My name is Evans, Arthur Evans. I've been digging around a bit in the Minoan ruins at Knossos." We shook hands. "For what it's worth, Mr. McCracken," said Evans, "I want you to know that I believe you, and—" he smiled, and there was the hint of a tear in his eye, "and I envy you. If ever the two of you feel inclined, please join me at my villa. I'd be happy to show you around the palace." Nodding to Ari, he left too.

Ari looked up at me for a long moment, and there was sympathy in her eyes. "Well, what did you expect?" she asked. "Never get involved in politics. I think you told me that once. In Rio."

"The fools," I ranted. "War will break out, millions will die. The orichalcum could prevent war from happening."

"When war comes," said Ari, opening the door so that we both stepped out into the bright sunshine, "it'll come whether we have the orichalcum or not. These people work on different principles from us—we can't make an alliance with them. They'll make war happen. They want it. We have to trust God that He will bring some good out of it." We were walking towards the Daimler, and Fritz was holding the door open for us. I fumed as we walked, while Ari watched me narrowly.

"I thought the Horn of Tempests would convince them of something."

"So did I," admitted Ari, "but to them, it was nothing but a vacuum cleaner. One of them actually suggested I use it to clean the house."

"I'm surprised he's still alive," I commented.

"He wasn't here today," she replied. "I heard he was sick."

"It just seems I've come out of this with nothing—absolutely nothing," I said. "I even lost the fire stone Dad gave me. I've got less than I started out with."

Ari linked her arm in mine. The bright Mediterranean sun glinted off the plain gold ring on her third finger. "Oh, I wouldn't say that, exactly," she said. Then, thoughtfully, she added, "When the war comes, we have to be ready to do our part to resolve it. There'll be plenty for us to do in the next few years." With that, she reached up and kissed me on the nose. "Come on," she said, "I'll buy you a drink."

THE END

Königsberger Klopsch

Ingredients

½ lb ground beef
½ lb ground pork
8 medium-sized potatoes
2 eggs, slightly beaten
1 medium onion, finely chopped
¾ cup fine plain breadcrumbs
½ cup flour
3 tbsp capers
2 cups chicken stock
1 lemon

¼ cup milk
½ cup sour cream
2 tbsp melted butter
2 tbsp cider vinegar
¼ cup dry white wine
1 tsp salt
½ tsp ground black
    pepper
5 black peppercorns
1 bay leaf

Directions

1. In a large saucepan or, heat chicken stock, bay leaf, cider vinegar, white wine, peppercorns, and 1 tbsp capers to a simmer over medium heat.

2. Meanwhile, combine beef, pork, eggs, breadcrumbs, milk, onion, juice of ½ lemon and 2 tbsp of capers, chopped; mix well.

3. Form meat mixture into golf-ball sized balls. Roll them in flour, and carefully place into hot broth, 10-12 at a time; simmer each batch for 15 minutes, but do not boil.

4. Carefully remove meatballs from the hot broth with a slotted spoon, and keep them warm. Discard bay leaf.

5. Peel, cut up, and boil potatoes
6. Stir juice of ½ lemon and sour cream into hot broth and heat through, but do not boil.
7. Add the cooked meatballs to the heated sauce, stir gently and warm through.
8. Serve meatballs with potatoes and Rotkohl

Rotkohl

Ingredients

4 slices of bacon, cut up into pieces about one inch square
1 red onion, finely chopped
1 tsp ginger
1 tsp cinnamon
1 large red cabbage, finely shredded
1 tsp marjoram
1 tsp salt

½ tsp black pepper
½ tsp cardamom
⅓ cup red wine vinegar
½ cup brown sugar
1 bay leaf
1 whole clove
1 apple, chopped

Directions

1. In a large saucepan, fry the bacon over a low heat for about 10 mins.
2. Add the onion, ginger, and cinnamon, increase the heat to medium, and cook, stirring occasionally, for about 5 mins.
3. Add the cabbage, stirring and cooking about 10 mins.
4. Add marjoram, pepper, cardamom, vinegar, bay leaf, clove and chopped apple.
5. Reduce heat to medium-low and simmer for 1 ¼ hours, stirring occasionally. It will stick a little, but do not worry about that, *Herren und Frauleins.*

6. Remove lid and cook, stirring frequently, for about 15 mins.
7. Stir in the brown sugar and cook another 15 mins.
8. Remove bay leaf before serving.

For dessert recipes, please check Fritz's page on the McCracken Books website, www.mccrackenbooks.com.

About the Author

 Like the famous Cat, Mark Adderley was born in Cheshire, England. His early influences included C. S. Lewis and adventure books of various kinds, and his teacher once wrote on his report card, "He should go in for being an author," advice that stuck with him. He studied for some years at the University of Wales, where he became interested in medieval literature, particularly the legend of King Arthur. But it was in graduate school that he met a clever and beautiful American woman, whom he moved to the United States to marry. He has been teaching writing and literature in America ever since, and now teaches for the Via Nova Catholic Education Program in South Dakota. He is the author of a number of novels about King Arthur for adults, and originally wrote the McCracken books for his younger two children.

Made in the USA
Middletown, DE
22 May 2021

39718734R00116